OUTCASTS

OUTCASTS

JOE L. HENSLEY

WILDSIDE PRESS
Berkeley Heights, NJ • 1999

WILDSIDE PRESS
P.O. Box 45
Gillette, NJ 07933-0045

This book is for Joseph M. Cooper, a one-of-a-kind lawyer.

OUTCASTS

CHAPTER 1

A BEGINNING

Any person with knowledge of politics in my state knew that the town of Avalon was United States Senator (once Governor) Bratewell's hometown. If I'd chanced to forget it there was a large reminding sign standing near the edge of the highway at the city limits. It read: "Avalon, Pop. 11,235. Home of U.S. Senator Eugene Bratewell."

Bratewell and I'd met during my lone term as a state legislator. Thereafter, when my then partner, who'd once been a state senator and who'd belonged to Bratewell's political party, had died, Bratewell had come calling at the funeral home. Mostly because of that final visit I'd decided to make a courtesy call upon his office before I got on with the real reason for my Avalon visit, which was a murder. I therefore stopped, got the four-year-old LTD filled with semi-precious gas, and obtained directions from the filling station attendant.

"Straight on six or seven blocks," he said. "You can't miss it." He inspected my out-of-town plates dourly. "You wouldn't be another big city reporter like some of them who've been writing that dirty stuff on the Senator now, would you?"

I shook my head.

"Okay," he said, mollified.

"Papers been picking on him some?" I asked curiously.

He nodded. He was a solid man with a thin face shadowed under the bill of an oil-stained cap.

"They ain't going to give him no chance," he said. "They've got together and bad wrote up everything he ever did. They've picked on his taxes, on his family, on the local hotel and his connections with it. If a crook ever stayed at the hotel they've tied him to Gene." He watched me. "You know the Grand Hotel?"

I nodded. I knew it.

"They write he and his people party too much at the hotel. They hint he chases women, but he don't and the town knows it. They say coal owns him and oil owns him. They say he talks one way in Washington and another back here at home." He shook his head and reluctantly accepted my money, sorry to lose his audience. "Gene's all right in my book. He ought to be the next President no matter what them polls say. He'd straighten things out in Washington."

"Sure," I said. It was all right with me. From the little I'd read I didn't think it had much chance of happening, but it was okay if it worked out that way.

"You know Major Potts?"

He nodded. "Sure. He used to come in here some."

"Where's he living now?"

"I ain't seen nothing of him for a while, but he ain't dead, mister. I'd of heard that. And it won't do either of us any good to try looking him up in the phone book. You know Potts don't believe in phones. He likes to talk to people when he can see their faces." He grinned, showing tobacco-flecked teeth. "Here now. You let me clean off your windshield." I was suddenly someone to be polite with.

I waited while he wiped away the road film. When I left he waved a genial good-bye to me.

I drove on down the street until I saw a sign for Bratewell's office. I parked and kicked my way through the late October leaves. The trees were getting bald. What leaves there were still on them wore good-bye colors. It seemed to me that a week ago it had still been golfing summer.

Bratewell's Avalon office wasn't large, but I supposed he kept his main in-state office in the state capital. I entered and found others waiting, some sitting and staring, others laboriously filling out papers. Two large men guarded an inner door. They sat on either side of it and watched us all suspiciously. I thought I remembered one of them, a mean state police officer who'd once guarded Bratewell as governor. The other guard was larger and younger. He fiddled with a belt holster, trying to make the gun it held comfortable around his substantial middle.

A crisp lady of middle years also looked familiar. She sat at a reception desk. She smiled inquiringly up at me.

"My name's Don Robak," I explained apologetically. "I think it would be enough if you'd just tell the Senator that I stopped by to say hello . . ."

"You were in one of his legislatures," she said brightly. "I remember your face. I'm certain he'll want to see you."

"He's here?" I asked.

"The Senator flew in last night. Yesterday he was the principal speaker at a fund raiser in Virginia. This afternoon he's supposed to cut the ribbon on a new mid-state bridge. Tonight he's scheduled to speak at a dinner in Minnesota. You sit down and wait," she ordered.

I obediently took a seat on a bench and tried not to watch the bodyguards at the door. I'd recently heard Bratewell's name mentioned now and then on television and read some accounts in my local paper concerning him as a long shot

presidential possibility. People around the country were form-
ing committees and trying to raise money to support him. I
remembered him as a competent, if uninspired, governor and
as an ambitious politician.

I sat.

It was not quite half an hour before the receptionist got
back to me. She answered a buzz at her desk and beckoned
me. She took me past the door guards.

Bratewell looked good, about the same as when I'd known
him as governor. He wore a vested, dark suit, a white shirt,
and the tie of a conservative. Two more guards were in his
room, both watching me. Bratewell waved reassuringly at
them, got up from behind a huge desk piled with papers, and
came around to meet me, hand outstretched. He smiled a
thousand-watt smile. He was medium-tall, slim, an impressive
man who made old and young female hearts beat faster. He
was very charismatic, a natural politician with a memory for
names like few I'd ever known. He was even middling hon-
est, or had been as governor.

"There you are, Don Robak," he said fondly. "I've not seen
you in three or four years, but I've read some things about
you in the papers. How's it going? How's the practice?" He
shook my hand and appraised me like a jeweler looking over a
suspect gem. "And what are you doing away from your Bington?"

"Business of sorts," I said, smiling in return. "I wanted to
stop past and say hello."

"Hello," he said, still smiling.

"I hear you've got big things going?"

He stopped smiling for the moment. "It all really starts
next year and I'm late into it. Right now it's just trying to get
committees going in the various states, get some organization,

keep my throat unsliced. Right now I'm a lightweight among heavyweights. The odds are against me, but it's a bet I mean to make."

I shook my head in wonderment. Down the years I'd known other governors, other U.S. senators, but he was my first presidential candidate.

"Someone has to do it, Don," he said insistently. "This country's going to hell. It's like a slide. The further you drop, the faster you drop. Governor Tighe can't win. He sounds like and is a flaming liberal. Grantham's too old and too sick to campaign. The rest will fall. My hope is that they'll come to me soon or late."

"This has to have your little town of Avalon on its ear, I'll bet," I said.

He nodded absently, intent on me. He asked, "Would you help me, Don?"

"I'm not into politics anymore, Senator. I haven't run for any office since the legislature."

"Sure. But you were once good at it and could be again," he said, retooling my reply into an agreement. He reached in his pocket and handed me a small badge. It was brass and would fit on a lapel. "Gene," it read. I smiled down at it and put it agreeably into my pocket.

"You look thinner," he said, perhaps to end the serious moment.

"I run a lot and I don't have lobbyists buying my meals nowadays." I looked him over again. "I wish I knew your tailor."

He nodded, smiling even more now. "I never divulge that name." He watched me curiously. "What sort of business brings you to Avalon?"

"My mother was a Hunter. Sam's my cousin."

He nodded and took a perceptible shuffle step backward. "I thought there was something I remembered. You told me once that you'd lived here as a boy?"

"Yes. They asked me to come over and look around and assess it," I said.

His eyes fell away from mine. "That should be an adventure for you. You have a certain reputation. Do you know that?"

"I know it."

"You've had a lot of publicity. That means the newspapers will be here when the trial starts."

"I suppose they will, if I defend it. They might be anyway."

He nodded. "Some of the people involved, including Sam Hunter, have been close to me, are close to me now. The Wyman girl's death has got my town riled up. Your relatives will tell you that."

"I've only heard a little bit about it—what my aunt Maude told me on the phone, then what I could find in the newspapers. I thought maybe I could hear more about it over here." I waited, hoping he'd offer.

I could almost see him adding and subtracting things. The days when he'd been governor and I'd been a useful member of the legislature were long past for both of us. He'd gone on to greater things and I was now only a lawyer who sometimes got press coverage because I defended sensational murders. Former State Senator Adams, now deceased, and once my partner, had been his real friend, not me. I was just someone from the opposition party who'd come along, made a small splash, and whom he'd therefore known.

"Don't know anything which would be of use to you, Don boy. Sorry, not a thing."

I waited, somehow hoping there might be something.

"I hope the upcoming trial and your being in it doesn't tear up my town too much. It's a good town. Sam was once a good man. I'm sorry for him now." He shook his head and looked restlessly at his watch. His guards stirred, sensing it was time for me to leave. Perhaps glancing at his watch was a prearranged signal.

"Thanks for stopping past," he said amiably. "It's good to see you again. I'd certainly like your help and could use you if you'd be willing to help me. Think about it, please." He shook my hand vigorously again.

In a few moments I was back on the street. I shuffled my way again through the fallen, crisp leaves. It was still warm and the sun was almost oppressive, but I could smell things dying. That morning, driving in, it had been autumn cold and clear as a whistle.

I knew I'd experienced a subtle bum's rush. I dropped my "Gene" brass badge into a pile of faded leaves.

Down from the cell Sam Hunter occupied, through the bars, I could see only one other prisoner. He sat on his jail cot carving designs in the soft, dingy plaster of his cell wall with what looked like a sharpened spoon. He saw me watching and stopped for a moment, then shrugged and went back to it intently, a true artist.

Sam Hunter said, "I guess I'm in a tight box, Don, but I didn't kill Sheila Wyman. I appreciate Maude calling you to take a look and help out." He clenched his huge hands and shook his head. He was a massive man, two years older than me. His hair was still almost completely black. He shook his head. "There isn't a lot to pay you with."

"How about a polygraph, a lie detector?" I asked, thinking of that for the first time.

"I took a poly at the state police barracks. A guy who used to be a friend gave it to me. I admitted hitting her a little so that showed up. I said she wasn't hurt any way that I could tell when I left her room and it showed I believed I was telling the truth on that. When I got asked if she could have maybe died from my smacking her my negative answer came in inconclusive." He shook his head. "Didn't do anyone much good." He leaned forward a little. "Did you hear me tell you there's nothing much to pay you with?"

"I heard. We'll talk about that more if I wind up doing anything substantial for you. The main thing is that if I stay I run things. I make the decisions and you abide by them."

"Okay by me, but just don't slow things down. Make them try me. It's set for next month."

"I may have to slow it down as a part of the defense, Sam."

After some thought he finally nodded. *"Try* not to slow it down."

"I'll try, but again, I make the decisions."

"Sure, sure." His eyes left mine and I could tell he didn't completely like me running the show.

We were cousins and old acquaintances. When Mom had sickened she'd left my father and come back to Avalon to die. She'd lasted a long, terrible year. I'd spent that final year with her in Avalon, a new kid in the small high school, a stranger. After I'd known she was dying it hadn't been an easy year. Sam, in his way, had helped.

Sam said, "I used to read about you now and then in the newspapers when I was still on the police force. I lost track, other than that. You quit coming here for reunions and things."

I had quit coming. Somehow Bington had become my town and I'd avoided both Avalon and the steel town far to the north where my robust father had lived out most of his chaotic life. But I'd kept up some on Avalon doings. I knew that Sam had once been a detective on Avalon's small police force, but had lost his job when the administration in city hall had changed. He'd been booted back to patrolman and been too proud to accept the demotion. I knew he had a wife and a child/children in the town. I'd met and known his wife. I thought for a moment: *One child, a boy.*

I also knew Sam had somehow acquired a young girl friend, that she'd been found savagely beaten to death in one of the buildings of the huge resort Grand Hotel, and that her brother was baying hotly after Sam's blood because of her murder and perhaps because of other things from my/our youth.

For the past half hour Sam had been trying to explain to me what had happened without giving me much information of legal value.

"I don't know your town anymore, Sam. I might wind up being a hindrance," I said carefully, giving him a chance to get off and let me off the hook.

He shook his head. "You know a lot of the people involved. It was Jeb Wyman's sister they say I killed. You probably wouldn't remember her, but you knew him. Some tell that I killed her because of Moll."

I remembered Moll. She was Sam's long-dead sister. And I remembered Jeb. When I'd known him he'd been a tall, bony boy, very good with a basketball, spoiled by stardom. I recalled he'd been cool to me at first, unwilling to accept me just because I was Moll and Sam's cousin. But I'd been around and underfoot and because of Moll he'd been careful not to show open dislike. Eventually he'd picked at me enough so that the fight which started looked like it was my doing. I'd not had my full growth then and he'd won the fight, *sort of*, but I'd smacked him around enough so that thereafter he'd grudgingly put up with or ignored me. *Until Moll died.*

"There's a town out there hating me," Sam said. "They ran me off the police force."

"How'd they do that?" I asked. Getting someone off the police force wasn't that easy. It was about like firing a teacher with tenure.

"I knew too much for them. I got wise to who was coming in for the high stakes gambling and I knew which hotel girls were selling it. I knew about the drugs and the Sunday booze and the skin shows. So they loaded some stuff in my locker at the station and then 'found it.' They told me I could quit or get fired. So I quit. Maybe I shouldn't have done it, but I did. After they kicked me down I kept writing letters to newspapers about what was going on at the hotel. I called people I knew, radio and newspaper and television. The hotel had to get rid of me. Now I'm in here."

"What is it about the hotel which bothers you so much, Sam?"

He shrugged, perhaps not really knowing. His answer was halting and confused: "It's just that they seem to know that they can get away with—do—damn anything and the town will take it. Somehow I know that's why I'm in here and why Sheila's dead. No other reason. Big money, Don. There's big money," he finished darkly.

"There's also a dead girl," I said. "You admit you were with her the night she died. You don't know anyone who had anything against her. You admit you fought with her, struck her.

What else is there? What's there for me? How about witnesses?"

He shrugged. "A couple of hotel employees saw us together in her room on that night before she was killed. We ordered up some food. A black waiter brought it. Then Wanda Shefel came past and borrowed twenty bucks from Sheila."

"Wanda Shefel?"

"She and Sheila were sort of friends. She's gone back to Chicago, but they tell me she'll come here for the trial." He shook his head. "She can't hurt me."

"Anyone who puts you in that room that night can hurt you."

"I was there, but I didn't kill Sheila," he said.

"Okay. What did this Wanda Shefel do at the hotel?"

"Worked as a waitress. Peddled herself now and then. Gave it away some, too."

"A prostitute?"

He shook his head. "She said once she was brought up in church, but the pill had set her free."

"Okay, let's move on. What about time of death. What do they have on that?"

"There was a call to the police. Some anonymous person claimed they'd heard a fight going on. The police came to check it about twenty or thirty minutes after I'd left." He nodded at me. "She wore one of those little watches around her neck. The crystal was broken and the watch stopped at ten thirty-five." He shook his head. "They'll be all excited about that watch setting the time of Sheila's death, but that watch never kept time worth a damn. She wore it because it was gold and had some diamonds in it. It was pretty, but useless. Like her, maybe."

"If she was useless why were you fooling with her?"

He smiled. He was a physical man, but he was not stupid. "Maybe because I'd gone useless, too."

"Okay. I'll check on the watch when I need to. How about written statements? Have you signed anything?"

He shook his head. "I haven't said anything they can use. They had those other witnesses and so they had me in her room and with her, but I told them I left before ten-thirty." He nodded. "I took off across the golf course for home."

I nodded sourly. He might not think that what he'd said meant anything, but I knew it could. In most trials there'd be different times in the evidence. Variances. No one would remember things exactly the same as other witnesses. But the more times they put Sam close to her on the night Sheila died, the tougher the case would grow.

"Did you sign some kind of statement on that?" I asked. "I mean about the time you left?"

He nodded.

"Don't sign anything else. Don't talk to anyone they put in jail about the case. Don't say anything about the case at all to anyone without me being with you. Understand?"

"All right," he said. "There's another thing. The deal on the poly was that both sides had to agree before it could be used or *any* of the answers given during it be used."

I nodded, not satisfied about that. "Did you write out some kind of agreement?"

"I didn't sign anything."

I smiled, wondering where the snakes would come from. Some people, even including police officers, suffer from extreme gullibility when arrested for a crime. They become their most damning witnesses.

"You say lots of people were after you? Anyone other than Grand Hotel people?"

"Mostly it was them," he said, unwilling to give up any paranoia on the hotel. He clenched his huge hands together. His strength was an Avalon legend.

"They hate me bad. They're real nice about it now, polite and all. My guess is they don't want the town to see them like they really are. So they're being cute and laughing up their sleeves and waiting it out and thinking they've got it made." He nodded. "Maybe they have."

"Tell me again about quitting the police force, Sam."

"They knocked me back to patrolman. When I wouldn't quit talking they put me on the parking meters. When that didn't work they put some Mary Jane in my locker."

"Who put it there?"

"Someone."

"You let them set you up and make you quit because of some marijuana in your locker?"

He nodded.

"You gave up your retirement?"

"Sure. It was fourteen years. But I got lump-summed. I got the money." He smiled, remembering. "I used it up—used it all."

"Chasing that girl?"

He stared ahead for a moment. Finally, he nodded.

I waited.

"I know you don't owe me nothing, but you're related to us Hunters on your mother's side and you know about Jeb and Moll and what he done to her and how she died. You know us all. When your mom knew it was her time she came back here to Avalon. Maybe you will too." He nodded at me again, very intent.

He'd been sort-of-kind to me that long ago year. I kept remembering and it got in my way, made me unable to be ra-

tional about his situation. I'd been the kid brought along because there was no place else. I'd been a bookish boy, content
then to hide behind novels about knights, Roman gladiators,
cowboys, and bug-eyed monsters. The first building I'd looked
for in Avalon was the library. I'd not known at first that Mom
was dying. Sam and his mother and father, Judge Hunter,
had taken us in, fed us, partially accepted us.

Sam had been the ultimate tyrant of that stage of my boyhood, a despotic bully who'd ruled my world, immensely
strong, completely king of his and my world. But he'd been
fair in his way. He'd let me, even forced me, to fight those
fights I could (or he thought I could) handle, but he'd pro-
tected me from all but his own bullying otherwise. I'd been a
new toy for him, the younger brother he'd never had, and so
the relationship had been beyond mere cousin friendship.
He'd been my ally.

The debts of adolescence, like those incurred in politics, are
nebulous things. *Then,* I'd have done whatever he suggested.
Now was a different time, inhabited by an older (wiser?)
Robak.

"You've got to promise me you'll stick around for it," Sam
said. "There was a big article about you recently in *The Capital Times.* They called you an 'attorney for the damned,' and
they said lots of people you'd beaten said you were just a
damned attorney. They said you knew about power and how
to use it. I liked it. I cut it out and carried it for a while. That
paper gets read lots around here. It'll scare them."

"Who will it scare?" I asked curiously.

"Scare Jeb. Scare the rest. I know they're walking cocky
right now, even if it was Jeb's sister." He shook his head.
"You check. He didn't care about her, believe me. I know he
didn't. And she hated him."

"I'll stay for a while and look around. And I'll come back for what needs doing in court. But I can't live here all the time while this is going on. I've got a practice in Bington and partners who are overworked. But I did tell them and Jo that I might be gone for a few days and I would like to see Aunt Till and Aunt Maude while I'm here."

"Who's Jo?" Sam asked.

"A lady I'm planning on marrying."

He shook his head at that, but then got back to his own situation. "Till ain't real well. And remember not to pay any attention to what she says about me. She hasn't had much use for me since I left Kate."

I nodded.

"You get hold of my lawyer soon. His name's Ellsworthy. He's maybe a hundred years old and he ain't much, but him and Pop were good friends so maybe he won't sell me out to the hotel. You can stay at my house. No one's there. Katie moved out when she filed her divorce papers."

"Katie's filed for a divorce?"

He nodded. "I don't blame her. She's too good for me. I want the best for her. I wish her good things." He gave me a careful look. "She's supposed to come sit by me at the trial. She didn't tell it to me direct, but my boy said she told him to tell me." He shook his head. "Katie don't come to the jail." He stopped and looked away. Out the cell door there was a high, barred window. You could see some sky and part of a tree. "Aunt Till or Aunt Maude will have the key to my house. They've been looking after the place since I've been in here."

"How about Senator Bratewell? I stopped past his office when I got to town. Where does he stand?"

Sam shook his head. "As far away from it all as he can get.

Ellsworthy told me that Bratewell once called to ask about me. Once we were friends." He shook his head. "He's a cautious man."

Something about his attitude bothered me. The Sam I'd known as a boy now seemed subdued—tamed.

"You're very complacent about being in here," I said.

He shrugged. "It's punishment. I was bad to Kate. I needed to be punished for that to make it right. But I didn't kill Sheila Wyman, Don." He shook his head, perhaps not sure. "We fought a little is all."

CHAPTER 2

THE RELATIVES

I drove the LTD into a back alley and parked behind a familiar-appearing old shed in a grassless pull-off spot. The doors to the shed hung limply open and it was empty. Half a block away, seen through gaps between houses, was the city park, three blocks long, an almost double wide block across. It would be a good place to run for exercise if I got to that.

I moved the other way, inside a wooden low gate with a latch lock. I found the decaying walk which became a gangway between two houses. The house I remembered best was medium in size, brick, and old. The house next north was also of brick, but it was a far larger and more imposing house. I walked to the end of the gangway. Inside the gangway the noise of my footsteps was magnified. At its exit all sound became normal again.

Two elderly ladies rocked sedately on the long, concrete porch of the larger house, taking the fine fall air. Both of them eyed me suspiciously.

"Afternoon Auntie Till, Auntie Maude," I said, feeling as if I was stepping twenty-five plus years back into my past. They seemed to have changed only a little. I'd grown mysteriously older, but they'd somehow remained as I remembered them from boyhood.

"You come on up here, Donald Robak," Auntie Till ordered imperiously.

I used their brick walk which I'd once weeded. I went up on the porch. When I drew closer to them I could see they both had changed. Maude seemed heavier. The flesh hung in unhealthy folds from her jowls and arms. Her dress was tentlike and her eyes were half closed, as if staying awake and alive was a chore. Till was toothpick thin, little more than stringy meat and warped, old bones. She smiled at me without humor, exposing yellowed false teeth.

"I guess we know what brought you," she said unpleasantly.

"I told you I wrote and asked him to come," Maude said.

"Sam told me one of you would have his house key. I'm to stay there while I'm in town," I explained. I waited, shuffling my feet. I remembered shuffling my feet the last time I'd been on their porch. Till had that effect on me still. Even though she seemed thin and ill she still radiated the illusion of being in control of her world. She wore thin, gold-rimmed spectacles. Sometimes, I remembered, she negligently forgot to pull them down from their nest in her bun of yellow-white hair. I'd thought, as a boy, she saw about as well without them as with them. She'd been, in the days when I'd been partially under her thumb, a precise lady who'd brooked no arguments with her pronouncements, her own supreme court. She might not always be right, but I could not recall her ever admitting to being wrong.

Both of them were very saving, even penurious. They salvaged all—string, tinfoil, old grocery sacks, bottles, aluminum cans.

Till had read her Bible openly and a lot when I'd lived close, but I suspected her reading was for show. She belonged to no church and preached her own Bible interpretations, wanting those she disliked to move directly to hell, sure she could accomplish it by her loud, angry, and public prayers.

I remembered a dozen things about her as I watched her. I remembered, with an odd taste in my mouth, that when Mom had died some pieces of cheap costume jewelry had vanished from her room, with Till or Maude the only person who could have removed them.

Yet they'd been good to Mom. They were her aunts. Her own parents were dead.

I remembered that Till's quiet, oppressed husband had still been alive when I'd come with Mom to Avalon. I'd sent him Christmas ties for a few years after I'd been taken back north to the steel town. After his death I'd gotten those ties back as gifts from Till at Christmas, one a year, some of them in what looked to be the same boxes in which I'd originally sent them.

Ah, well.

We'd become estranged after I'd reached maturity. First of all I was (gasp) divorced. Till didn't believe in or accept the law of divorce. Second, and perhaps more important, I'd not come to Avalon to practice law. She'd bade me do that, possibly so she could enjoy free legal services. When I hadn't appeared there'd been a series of plaintive notes and then, finally, stony silence.

But today she seemed at least willing to see me, and Aunt Maude, fat and phlegmatic, seemed actually glad. I remembered that Maude had led a difficult life. She'd been widowed young, had to go to work, had endured sicknesses and lost both of her sons in wars. She was, nevertheless, the more human of the two old women. Long life together, however, had made them much alike.

I sat in a vacant rocker. There were half a dozen of them on the porch. We rocked together for a time.

"Tell me first about Sam and Katie," I said.

Aunt Till shook a disapproving head. "After the job was gone he got to drinking like a desert dog. He met that tarty little Wyman girl sometime soon after. I think he saw a good chance to get back at Jeb Wyman for the loss of his job and for Moll."

"What did Jeb have to do with Sam losing his job?"

She smiled coldly. "Jeb runs politics in this town. He had a finger in it somehow, you can bet. Them two boys was best friends when they were boys until that night Moll fell screaming over the cliff out at the state park. She was supposed to be with Jeb. Sam has hated Jeb for that ever since." She looked at me. "You know that's so, Donald."

I nodded. "I know it," I said. Jeb had not even been close to the accident spot when Moll had fallen to her death, but he'd been her date that night (and every night) and that had been enough for Sam to hold him responsible.

"So here was Jeb's baby sister, fifteen years younger than Sam and Jeb. And Sam, out of a job, drinking a lot, handsome and mean. There maybe got to be more than Moll to it for Sam. That Wyman gal chased him hard. After Katie moved out and took the boy along Sheila Wyman would come right to the house next door and use the key Sam had given her, bold as a bank bandit, painted and pretty, little, pug nose all flared out and ready. She had a big Cadillac car and plenty of money. Still the town out there believes Sam killed her mostly on account of Moll. At least a lot of them do." She nodded her head and sniffed. "There was a time when I could have told you how many for certain, but very few people talk to us Hunters these days."

"Where'd Katie go?"

"Back to her dad's farm. He'd been dead five years last August. She took the boy along with her. I've seen him come to visit his dad a couple of times at the house and they say he goes to the jail, but I've not seen hide nor hair of Katie." She shook her head dolefully. Katie had been her favorite. I remembered that. Kate had been Sam's girl as far back as my memories of Avalon went, even before Mom had brought me tagging behind her into her family town.

Maude gave me a harsh look. "Sam killing that little tramp is the worst thing that's ever happened in Avalon. This town will never forget it, never forgive him, or the whole Hunter family for that matter. You listen. You'll hear it."

"It sounds like Sam's case ought to be tried in another town," I said. "I'll have to talk about that with Sam's local counsel."

Till smiled at Maude. "Ed Ellsworthy? He hasn't made a decent decision about anything since before World War Two. He'll bumble in and tumble out. Only reason Sam hired him is he's cheap. And you can bet Ed hears the town around him. He won't do anything to really add hisself to the unpopular list." She examined me. "So you're really going to represent him, then?"

I shrugged and then nodded. I could see she didn't like me being there, but that was all right. I said, "I told him I would help him. I'm going to look around some first."

"Well look then." She turned the other way in her chair, toward Aunt Maude. Maude suddenly seemed asleep. Her eyes were closed.

"Get him the key, Maude," Till ordered.

Maude apparently slumbered on. I could hear the sound of her breathing.

"Fat old fool," Till muttered, not really angry about it. She reached out and found a heavy cane at the side of her rocker. She'd affected one since I could first remember seeing her. Now, she seemed to need it. She got up with difficulty. Her Bible, which I'd not seen but suspected, almost fell from her chair. She caught it and placed it back on the rocking seat.

"You wait here," she ordered.

I rocked on in my chair and waited. On this side and the other side of Main Street there were other huge, old houses, block after block of them. One of them belonged to Senator Eugene Bratewell, but I couldn't remember which one. I did remember that Till held Bratewell in minor contempt. To her he was a Johnny-come-lately, a relative newcomer to Avalon, whose family wasn't *that much*. She could not forgive him his ancestors or his political success with the "wrong" party.

In a while she came shuffling back with a big, old-fashioned key and a smaller one for a newer lock. She sat down in her chair without offering them.

"The small one's for the shed. You can park your car inside nights and lock the shed. Lots of vandals around the city park nights."

"All right."

"Did Sam tell you strangers tried to beat him up before he had to leave the police force?"

I shook my head, interested.

"Three men. They had clubs. They layed on him good," she said, smiling about it. "Broke some of his ribs. Sam hurt two of them and got away. Must have been out-of-towners. They never caught them."

"That's too bad."

She nodded. "Maybe so, maybe not. I'm just trying to make

sure you know what you're getting into. He's not your boss anymore."

"I know that."

"Someone shot through his bedroom window one night, too. That was when he was writing his letters to the newspapers. I guess the police figured it was someone who worked for the hotel or maybe some other boyfriend of Sheila Wyman's. Not that Sam didn't deserve trouble, leaving his wife and boy, drinking and carousing. He got in bad, years back, with those hotel people and you know the hotel runs this town. Jeb Wyman's on the board. He used to send local workers for the hotel to talk to Sam at first, acting like they were still Sam's friends. But that was a long time back." She looked away from me, up and down Main Street, seeing it all. She nodded, willing to make my decision for me. "You stay maybe a day or so and then move on. Come back for the trial if you must, but stay mostly away from it. Sam's made his own mess. He couldn't get along with the hotel, he lost his job, threw away his wife. He lived dirty with that girl. The town knows she was a tramp, but that won't save Sam. No way. He's straight and dead ahead on his road to hell. Nothing you can do." She nodded, not unsatisfied about it, but then she'd always had a puritanical streak.

I remembered something else. "Does Mrs. Wyman still live down the street a couple of blocks where she lived when I was here?" I asked.

"Lisa? Yes, she still lives in the old house. Jeb lives with her there after two divorces. Since the girl was murdered Lisa stays inside the house. I've not seen or heard about her being outside it. Some of the close neighbors say she acts crazy-like. I guess that would be no wonder what with Sam killing her only daughter."

"Sam's only accused, not convicted, Aunt Till. He says he didn't do it. Is Lisa Wyman so crazy that someone couldn't knock on her door and talk with her and make some sense of it?"

"You'd better stay away from her," Till advised ominously. "If Jeb caught you close he might just take a shotgun to you. He'd get away with it too in this town, what with you being Hunter related."

"What does our all-American Jeb do now for a living?"

"Sells most of the real estate in town. Plus he's big in politics, district chairman and moving up, I hear. And he's on the board of the Grand Hotel. When he was younger, before he got so heavy, I used to see him on television commercials, what with him being all-American in college."

Aunt Maude slept on, snoring gently now. Till regarded her and shook her head. "Since she got so fat all she does is sleep." She watched me wisely and made one of those statements which left me scratching my head. "She's too heavy for her weight."

I thought back to my boyhood. Then, Maude had seen the good side of all, Till, the dark. They'd bickered and fought and gossiped together for all the years I remembered. Maude lacked Till's strength and Till was, by far, the dominant personality, but they were incomplete without each other. I had a sudden moment of insight. Maude must know that Till was very sick. Perhaps Maude also no longer wanted to be well. Perhaps she tried to grow fat so that she might soon die. It seemed possible. The old are only children with years on them.

When I'd been a boy people had visited all the time on their jointly owned porch, but things were quiet now. Although people had passed on the street in front of us, no one

had waved, no one had called out or approached. Maybe it
was only a temporary thing, maybe not. Small towns have
ways of punishing not only malefactors, but also those close to
them.

I rocked on, thinking, watching the street. In a bit I noticed Till was dozing too. The keys had fallen from her hand
into her thin lap.

I rose and took them. Her old lizard eyes opened and saw
me, then wearily closed again. I realized again that she was
very sick.

I opened Sam's front door with the key. Inside things
smelled musty and stale. I dropped my bag in the tiny room
I'd occupied years before; a bed, a bureau, one tiny window.

Uptown, across the street from the limestone block city
hall, within sight of the Grand Hotel, I found the law office
of Edwin Ellsworthy, one flight up from the busy street. I
walked up squeaky steps and found a door with his name on
it down a dim hall.

I remembered Ellsworthy a little. He was an old cam-
paigner who took long walks, mostly at night. Some people in
the town of Avalon liked to gossip he window-peeped, but
he'd never been charged with it formally.

A sweet young thing worked at a typewriter, tongue caught
between teeth in concentration, perhaps trying to spell "cat"
or "dog" or one of those other tough ones. She raised her eyes
and looked me over, apparently trying to classify me. Was I
book salesman? Debt collector? Possible new client? She
smiled, not able to figure me out and I was glad I'd worn my
best Kingsridge suit.

"Can I help you?"

"Is Mr. Ellsworthy in?"

She nodded guardedly.

"My name's Robak. I'm a lawyer from over in Bington. I'd like to talk to him about the Sam Hunter case."

She smiled more at me and nodded. "I think he's been kind of expecting you. I didn't think you'd be so young."

"Thank you." I said.

She got up from behind her typewriter and entered another room. She came back to the door and beckoned me, still smiling.

"Mr. Ellsworthy will see you now."

I entered a large, impressive room. The walls were covered by row on row of law books, mostly case reports. The floor was thickly carpeted. There were two oversized windows. One looked out on city hall, the other on the main building of the Grand Hotel complex.

Ellsworthy shook hands limply. My heart fell a little as I inspected him. He now had to be almost eighty years old. He was thin and he breathed with wheezing difficulty. His eyes refused to meet mine. Abstracts cluttered his desk. He wore heavy glasses with a built-in hearing aid in one shaft.

"Catching up on work," he explained hoarsely. "The world can go to hell around us, but there'll still be bank work. Sam said you might come over." He shook his head disapprovingly. "That boy's in a bad way."

Ellsworthy was medium tall and stooped, probably from hauling land title books around damp recorder's offices.

"Nice to meet you, sir," I said in a low voice.

"Who's that?" he asked, not understanding.

"I said it's nice to meet you," I said loudly.

"No need to yell, young man," he answered sharply. "I hear well enough when people don't whisper." He sat down behind his desk and gestured me to a chair. "The prosecutor would deal this one for maybe twenty years. I'd take it if I could talk Sam into it."

"Should it be tried in Avalon?"

"I've suggested a change of county, but Sam won't hear of it. He wants it tried here." He nodded to himself. "Maybe he's right. He still has some friends, people who owe him favors. He's spent his life acting like a politician in an election year, tough on trouble makers and the hotel, but grinning at the rest of the world, playing the fool. A lot of people out there in Avalon probably still like Sam, but I'll wager most of them would find him guilty. It'll be hard not to get a jury that's unbiased. Maybe one of Sam's special friends could sneak onto it." He didn't seem hopeful about it, shaking his head. "Prosecutor ain't dumb and he's lived here all his life. He won't let that happen."

"How about discovery?" I asked.

He gave me a sour look. "Are you going to do the trial?"

"I imagine I will. I'd still want you to help picking the jury and maybe take some of the witnesses."

He smiled, visibly relieved. "I'll be glad to help where I can. As to that discovery business I just don't believe in it. If I start it then the state finishes it. I've defended a ton of cases and won lots of them without discovery. I already know who their witnesses are going to be. Without discovery they won't know ours."

I smiled and refused comment. Discovery was a useful tool. It not only got at the facts of a case, but also, after a time, tended to limit fact areas. Items not provided might not be admissible. And a *complete* list of state's witnesses and exhibits would give me a place to begin.

"Has Sam been arraigned?" I asked.

"Sure. All nice and neat. Day after he was formally

arrested. The grand jury met and indicted him. Sam got read his new warrant and I asked to have him arraigned. We've got a tentative trial date for middle of next month, if we can get ready by then." He looked me over again. "Say again how much help you want from me?"

"All I can get. In the trial I'll want you to do *voir dire*, jury examination, plus I'll maybe want you to examine some of the witnesses. Right now I want you to just sit tight. I'm going to be around town for a time. I'm going to ask some questions and figure out exactly what went on that night. Sam says he didn't kill her and I'm going to stay with that for a while." I thought for a moment. "Was there ever a bond hearing?"

"No. It seemed futile."

I didn't think "futile" would be the correct word. Petitions to let to bail, bond hearings, get the defense a chance to see what the prosecution has and what it's going to sound like in advance of the trial date.

"Maybe I'll want to file a petition for one," I said.

He shrugged, apparently not caring. "You ought to stop over and see Judge Cory and let him know you're in it with me. That's polite." He smiled and leaned back in his chair, lecturing me a little. "It's good to be polite with judges."

"I'm sure it is. I'll do that soon."

"If you're really in earnest about this discovery business you could dictate the papers to Linda." He cackled a little, thinking about that. "Then watch her. She's young and pretty, but she don't spell too good."

"The bond hearing would probably do as much for us," I said.

"Linda can give you my file in the case and you can look it over," he said. "There ain't much in the file. There is enough to let me know they've got a case. You look it over and then talk to Sam. Maybe we can get a good deal for him from the prosecutor." He looked back down at his desk, selected an abstract, and laid it where he could examine it.

"Thank you," I said.

He nodded brusquely, dismissing me.

"You still walk at nights?" I asked.

He looked up, startled. "A little. How'd you know about that?"

"I lived here for a time. Anyone around town giving you any problems on the case?"

"I had some crank calls right at first." He raised a hand to forestall other questions. "I've got to do this work now. You look around and then come back to see me. Call ahead."

In the outer office Linda did better than expected. There was a copying machine. She made me copies of the several papers in Ellsworthy's thin file. She gave me the small sheaf of copies. The indictment had the witnesses listed thereon. Better, there was a three-page copy of the police report.

With *all that*, I departed.

CHAPTER 3

THE HOTEL

If I wanted to direct someone from a far country to the town of Avalon I'd do it by telling them to follow the Grand Hotel signs, for Avalon was the Grand Hotel.

Avalon was located close to Indianapolis and within easy driving range of Cincinnati, not too far from Nashville, and in the vicinity of St. Louis, Louisville, and Chicago. Avalon was long miles from an interstate and there'd not been, for many years, any rail service.

Even so the town and the huge resort-convention hotel had survived and apparently prospered.

The Grand Hotel stood on the highest ground in Avalon, towering over the town. It was visible from the front or back doors or side windows of almost every downtown Avalon business building.

A hotel had stood on that choice hill sence the early 1800s with the present group of buildings by far the largest and most imposing. The first inn had been built by an itinerant merchant fresh off the muddy river that flowed at the south edge of Avalon. The merchant had sensed the value of the warm, smelly springs that bubbled to the hill surface there. He'd called the place Indian Lick after the Indians who for

centuries had come there to bathe and use the waters for medicine. That first small building had burned in 1829 and been
replaced by a larger, grander building which had also been
consumed by a fire in 1865. By then, if I remembered the
town gossip I'd heard as a boy, the hotel had already begun to
acquire a dark reputation. The often-whispered tale about
that second fire was that a soldier returning unexpectedly
from the Civil War had angrily set it after finding his wife
happily going wrong at the hotel. The third set of buildings
had been completed in 1871. One of those buildings still partially remained. In that often remodeled building Sam
Hunter had allegedly beaten Sheila Wyman to death after a
quarrel.

In addition to that older wing there was a huge assembly
area, four newer guest-room wings, covered and open walkways, two golf courses, four swimming pools, dozens of tennis
courts, half of them under roof for year-round play. There
were ski trails, a stable, a playground for children, plus a long
porch on the second floor of the main building with hundreds
of chairs to sit and talk and be seen in. Even Till, not an ar-
dent admirer of the hotel, had expressed admiration for that
porch.

I remembered that the hotel bought locally, contracted
with local artisans, employed townspeople to clean the rooms
and staff the dining rooms, hired mostly area men and women
to polish and cook and do the myriad jobs that needed doing.
The hotel paid a substantial share of the county taxes and
paid them early, if needed.

Hotel people and their families had sat on and controlled
most of the councils of the town when I'd been a boy, and I
thought I could assume that such continued.

It was the place to begin. I walked up there to see if something startling would happen when I asked to see the scene of the crime.

A marquee in front of the main building read: "Welcome Savings and Loan Associations." Arriving buses halted in the wide asphalt drive and disembarked gaudily clad men and women from a hotel-sponsored trip somewhere. It was now late afternoon.

A huge sign hanging above the porch read: "National Headquarters, Eugene Bratewell for President."

The police report, carefully read, had informed me in what room Sheila Wyman had been killed. I remembered the hotel well enough from boyhood and later bar conventions to know almost exactly where that room was, but I'd determined not to do anything the easy way. I wanted, and I'd sensed Sam also wanted, the town of Avalon and the Grand Hotel people to know someone else was checking, that the game had been subtly altered by the addition of a new person. I went directly to the main desk.

A handsome young desk clerk smiled at me. He wore a plastic badge on the lapel of his fashionable suit. "Louis—Four Years Serving You."

"I'd like to take a look inside room 1014A, Louis, if it's available."

"It's available. We don't rent it out these days and won't until things are done with."

"What things?"

"The trial I guess." He eyed me suspiciously. "Police? Reporter?"

"Lawyer," I explained. "I'm working for Sam Hunter." I found a card in my billfold and extracted it. I gave it to him. He accepted it gingerly.

"Mr. Ellsworthy represents Sam Hunter," he said. "I already showed him inside the room."

My opinion of Ellsworthy moved up a bit. I said, "Sometimes a person charged with a crime will decide to have more than one lawyer. It's legal. I can get a court order to see the room if you want, but I'll make some noise when I get it."

"You wait right here," he said, upset a little. He opened a door behind the front desk without knocking on it. I could see an office inside and part of an ornate desk before the door closed. Louis had taken my card in with him.

I waited. He came back in a few moments *sans* card. He fumbled down a row of pigeonholes and found a key.

"Bring the key back here when you're done," he ordered. "Will you need a bellman or do you think you can find the room?"

"I can find it. I used to live here in Avalon before I went straight."

He smiled politely, a professional smile.

Room 1014A was, as I'd thought, in the furthest, oldest section of the huge hotel. I used the back asphalt paths. They were now peopled with hotel guests dressed in their late afternoon finery off for a drink in one of the bars, then dinner. Some of them nodded and I nodded back.

The "A" section seemed mostly deserted. I found 1014 down a dimly lit hall and inserted the key. The door opened smoothly. At the outside window the curtain was open and it was light enough to see well.

I looked around. It seemed a typical enough room for the Grand. It was ground floor and the outside window was actually, I discovered, a sliding glass door which opened to a tiny patio and then exited to an outside, asphalt walk. I tried the sliding door. It was locked, but minor fumbling found the opening formula for me and I pushed it open noiselessly.

I got out the police report and read it again. When the police had arrived the sliding door had been partly open. There'd been no evidence its lock was forced. The only significant debris on the floor consisted of tiny bits of glass from Sheila's watch crystal. The night of the murder had been clear and dry.

Sam had told me they'd fought, made it up by making contesting, bitter love, then fought again. It had not been, according to him, an unusual thing for them to do. He remembered nothing about any damage to her watch. He did remember she'd gone savagely for his face with sharp nails and he'd slapped her to stop the attack. Some skin found under her nails, according to the police reports, matched Sam's. I could figure the state would have a bevy of experts testifying on that. Sam claimed he'd left by the sliding door, walked across the night-deserted golf course, and from there the few blocks to his home. He'd seen no one. She was alive and well and cursing him when he left. I shook my head, thinking on it. It was a simple case. Sam had left his coat behind and he'd admitted striking the girl. The coat had wound up spotted with Sheila's blood.

I remembered Sam's remarkable strength. He'd been, even as a young man, the kind who performed superhuman things. Once I'd seen him lift the front end of a small car from the ground. I remembered reading when he was a policeman about him walking into an in-progress bank holdup, absorbing two bullets, then beating his assailant into unconsciousness with his fists. I knew, from the time I'd spent in Avalon, that he wasn't a cerebral person. He wasn't stupid, but books and great thoughts weren't his way. He was a person who acted first and then thought on it. I shook my head.

I looked around again, trying to visualize things as they'd been that night, but no ideas came.

The room was twentieth century ordinary, genus hotel. There was a bath in the old style, perhaps left over from earlier times, a huge, claw-footed affair. There was an ornate marble washbowl and counter, a chrome and plastic shower stall. There were chairs and a table, lamps, two queen-size beds, and a center wall mirror above a bureau. I lifted the mirror a little and looked behind it, remembering a story I'd recently heard about a startled man who'd seen his own face starring in an X-rated, under-the-counter movie. The outer limits of evil in these times can also affect the unwary. The wall behind the mirror, when I tapped it, was solid.

Sheila Wyman had been found dead after someone made a complaining, anonymous call to the Avalon police. A call by whom? The wing had been unused that night. A passerby maybe? I shook my head. I have a suspicion of all things which appear to happen by coincidence. I supposed someone could have heard the fighting, someone could even have watched, but it seemed to me, if I wanted to believe Sam, that the same passerby could have been someone shadowy. Maybe it had been the killer who'd called, someone who'd watched and waited and found the right time and place.

Her face had been savagely beaten with what the police called "blunt force instruments." That could be anything, a club, a lead pipe, or something else. No weapon had been found and Sam's fists were the heavy favorites via the grand jury indictment. There'd been no further looking once Sam was in jail.

I wondered why Sheila and Sam had chosen this particular room.

Being a completist I even looked under the beds despite all the time which had passed since the date of the murder, now two plus months back. I also pulled out every drawer in the room and checked in back of them and under them, but there was nothing.

Sheila Wyman had been twenty-eight years old.

I locked the sliding door and exited the way I'd entered.

At the walk I turned toward the golf course and walked there, going the way Sam would have gone, I thought. A short walk brought me to a creek that divided the path from the golf course, but I found a wooden bridge. I stood on it and watched a late, hurrying foursome through.

A man riding in a mesh-covered golf cart drove slowly past. I thought he was probably a golf course employee. He stopped near the bridge and watched me for a time. When I ignored him he came to the bridge.

"Looking for someone?" he asked.

"Just looking."

"You a hotel guest?"

I lifted the key to 1014A out of my pocket and shook it.

He still was not satisfied and frowned a little. He was a thin, tall man with an acne-pitted face. The face and his manner made him seem tough and capable.

"You could get hit with a golf ball standing there," he warned.

"I'll watch carefully," I said.

He shook his head and drove away.

I got back to my looking. A man could cross the golf course here and be quickly on a city street. Sam undoubtedly had done it that way. A few more blocks to his house. An easy walk. No way to check.

Old memories came back. *Maybe there was. A chance.*

I walked back to the main building and turned the key in at the desk. Louis, the four-year veteran, smiled at me.

"Thank you, Mr. Robak." I saw him try to resist his urge, but be unable. "Find anything?" he asked sarcastically.

I smiled also. It was not the time to be compromising or easy. "I always find things, Louis. Enough to keep life interesting both for me and those I question in damp and drafty courtrooms. Thank you for the key. Did you, by chance, know Sheila Wyman?"

"Just vaguely. I knew who she was." He smiled. "I'm a married man."

"You've been most courteous."

He nodded and glanced anxiously toward the door behind him, eager to report.

I walked through the lobby and found a small bar near the main exit. It sat in the middle of a tiny mall of shops. I went into the bar and took a booth and ordered Early Times and water from a shapely waitress clad in almost enough clothes to constitute the legal minimum. She wrote the order down carefully, her tongue between her teeth, perhaps afraid she'd forget it in the ten-foot trip back to the bar. She was young, reasonably handsome, and ready to advise me.

"In a little while, when it gets dark," she said softly, "most of the action moves upstairs."

"Thanks. What sort of action would that be?"

She gave me a wise look. "Wine and women, honey." She went away and soon brought back my E.T. and water and patted my hand. "You try the Green Room, sweets."

"Is that maybe where Sheila Wyman used to work?"

"Did you know our poor Sheila?" she asked, suddenly wary of me.

"A little. One of the bellmen said something bad had happened to her." I smiled upward at all the view she afforded. "I think I used to see her around the Green Room."

"She never worked in there."

"Maybe, but she hung out there. That's where I met her. I'm certain of it. She was with some big, black-haired guy, lots older than she was." I looked up again to see how I was doing. My waitress had one Band-Aid on low and two more high and all three were covered with improbable black netting. When she'd walked away for my drink I'd spied a mid-air bunny tail in back. I was dizzy from the view.

"You never," she scoffed. "That could be the guy they're saying killed her. He used to be a bad news policeman around here."

"Bad news?"

"Lots of the guys who work here at the hotel didn't like him. The sports kind of guys."

"You mean the people who gambled?"

She nodded.

It seemed worthwhile to carry the conversation further with her, but I could see she was running out of time for me now.

I smiled at her. "How about you? What time do you get off work?"

"I got me a steady boyfriend, honey. He don't much like the idea of me working here in a bar in close to my birthday suit, but he's out of a job right now and we need the money. When quitting time comes he's always right outside in the parking lot drinking a beer and waiting, asking me questions, mad at the world." She patted my cheek gently, examining me, apparently approving (although I didn't know her standards). "Not that it might not be fun. Try the Green Room. You'll find some action there."

"All right," I said. "I'd like to come in here again and see more of you."

She smiled at my tired joke and I ordered a second E.T. and water. I saw her discuss my second drink with the bartender. He poured it and then absented himself from behind his bar.

In a little while, after I'd sipped my second drink down a few inches, a tall, gray-haired man came into the small bar. He was beautifully dressed, very distinguished looking, and perhaps sixty years old. He nodded authoritatively to the returned bartender and approached my table.

"I'm Roger Cowles, executive manager of this circus," he said, smiling easily at me. "I heard you were around. Can I sit down and talk with you for a few minutes?"

"Sure."

He sat. "We've told our people not to discuss the Hunter case or Sheila Wyman with anyone, Mr. Robak. There was a lot of publicity when it happened. It hurt our business for a time. So we soft-pedal it now. I'm sure when the trial comes along we'll get some lumps again, but there's no way around that." He nodded carefully. "Now, if there's a way we can help you, anything you want to know, we'll try to accommodate you. I want you to understand that the management of this hotel doesn't care whether Mr. Hunter's convicted or acquitted."

"That's hard to believe. I've heard Jeb Wyman's a member of your board of directors."

"Do you know Mr. Wyman?"

"Yes. From a long way back."

He frowned at my answer, perhaps not expecting it. "Mr. Wyman is a member of the board. He's one of seven members. I've seen nothing to indicate that he or any other board member want us to hide anything or do anything to impede or slow the case."

"I may slow it some," I said, watching for his reaction. "I'm fresh into it. I want to take a hard, new look at the whole picture, perhaps ask for a bond hearing before trial, take depositions, petition for discovery."

"We'll still try to cooperate, assuming you ask anything of us." He smiled ingratiatingly. "We'd still like to see it over and done with—and soon."

"I'm sure you would. To speed things I'd like to look over your records for the day of the killing and, if need be, the days before it. I'd like your calendar of events. I'd like to wander through your operation, then chase wherever I find leads."

"Something resembling that might be partly arranged," he said. "When do you want to start?"

"How about tomorrow?"

"You're very quick."

"It could be in your best interests that I am. If I get truly satisfied that Sam did it then I'll move on and things will proceed more routinely. Then my help for him will have to be an attempt at a plea bargain. So the quicker, the better. I have other business and not a lot of time," I said, watching, picking words out for his benefit.

He smiled and nodded. "Come by my office in the early afternoon."

"I may want to get into your operation here also."

"That's not so easy."

"How about if I just talk privately, on their time, with some of your employees?"

"That's all right. I doubt there's anyone around who can help you much."

"How's that?"

"There just weren't very many witnesses," he said. "Some people saw him at the room, some others saw them fight. But I've heard he's admitted that."

"I see."

"What I want you to see, Mr. Robak, is that we don't want trouble here, or perhaps it would be more correct to say we don't want any more trouble than we already have."

"Did Sheila Wyman ever work in your Green Room, Mr. Cowles?"

"The Green Room's a popular night spot here in our hotel. We try to get our best-looking girls there. Sheila was a handsome lady, but she worked in management. If she was ever in the Green Room it would have been as a visitor."

"Your waitress made it sound like quite a wild place."

"She's been told to do that. Right now, like at most times, the hotel's fighting to make a dollar. We do all right when we've got a convention in house, not so good when we don't. The Green Room has a stiff cover charge and gets double for drinks what we overcharge you here." He grinned. "There's a show of sorts, mostly area talent, and there's a piano bar before and after the show. It helps pay the bills."

"I may wind up trying it for murder," I said.

"I don't understand," he said, startled.

"I don't want to try Sam, assuming I continue in his case. I need an alternative to take a jury's mind off him. Sheila Wyman died here at your hotel and worked here at your hotel, Mr. Cowles. It seems possible to me that some deviate guest, attracted here by things like your Green Room and your semi-nude waitresses, passed by that night and observed Sheila Wyman, saw Sam leave, found the door open, and then entered and killed her."

"I see. It also sounds possible to me," he said tolerantly. "It doesn't sound good for my hotel business, but we'll have to try weathering it. I think we will. The town likes us. We hire their people and always have hired them. The Grand Hotel and Avalon have a long and enduring friendship."   .

"Sure," I said. "The problem for you isn't Avalon. You don't do your guest business with the town. You do it with conventions and honeymooners. Bad publicity costs money. Your guests at the hotel don't want to pay for rooms and entertainment and then take a chance on winding up dead at the hands of some wandering homicidal maniac."

"I understand you, but I don't think you understand me. I'm saying that to make your story fly you've got to make it plausible enough to run by local jurors who like the Grand Hotel and are friendly toward it. I wonder how you plan to get the job done?" He watched me and I thought I saw malice in his eyes.

"I'll worry about a jury after I try selling my version to the news media," I said carelessly.

"Selling it there won't do your client any good," he said, malice fading.

"Did you ever hear of a change of venue?"

"I've only heard that Sam's insisting on having his trial held in Avalon."

"I'll be the one who decides that," I said, without complete truth. "When I'm in a case I make all decisions. No one else makes them. People who hire me do as I say." I nodded convincingly. "Trials and appeals take a long time and they're

news. I'll be giving my views long after yours, assuming you
testify, are merely words in a transcript. So, until I find a better theory excluding Sam Hunter I'm stuck with what I im-
mediately see."

He nodded gloomily.

"How well did you know Sam?" I asked.

"I knew him some after he left the police force. I knew
who he was before. He was a nuisance then."

"I've heard he kept things in line in the town and here at
the hotel."

He shook his head. "Not really. He was like a college kid
at a panty raid. Avalon had lots of burglaries. I never knew
Sam to catch anyone there. It was easier for him to come
smelling around here." He smiled, remembering. "So they
fired him."

"Did you people help in that?"

"We didn't object."

It was difficult to fit Sam's job and Sheila's murder into a
single place in my mind. I shook my head, thinking. "Sheila
lived in town even though she worked for your hotel?"

"I suppose."

"Why'd she have a room out there in the old wing that
night?"

"Because she wanted it, I suppose. I don't really know, but
I'll bet our books will show she rented it legally." He sounded
positive.

"As a trysting place with Sam alone?"

He shrugged, unwilling to comment.

"How well did you know her, Mr. Cowles?"

"I knew her. I bought her a drink a time or two. As to
other men I can't tell you much. She was interested in men
and they were interested in her. I saw her with lots of men.

She drew them. She was good at her hotel job, bright and competent. She worked in catering, setting up banquets and meetings. If she hadn't been able to do the job, we'd not have kept her, brother on the board or no." He thought for a moment and then nodded. "Working around the hotel she'd have known how to get any room she wanted when the place wasn't booked full. I recall having some checking done on her for a police officer who asked similar questions. Someone on the desk checked it for him at my order."

"What police officer was that?"

"Lieutenant Hamilton. He was the investigating officer."

"State or local?"

"Local police," he said. "I never saw any state police. The local police did it all, not that it took long. They were quickly satisfied and sure it was Sam Hunter." He nodded, almost to himself. "The night Sheila died was a slow night around the hotel. Sheila rented the only room that was used in that whole wing. My guess is she wanted seclusion. I've heard around, rumors only, that she was after Sam to get his divorce and marry her." He looked down at his fine wristwatch and then got up. "I've talked too long. I've got to get back now. Come see me tomorrow. Within reason, I'll try to help."

"Maybe you'd better check with Jeb first?"

"I don't need to check with anyone."

"Where are you from, Mr. Cowles?"

"The East, originally. New York state. I got hired for this job from a hotel in Las Vegas."

"You must miss that when it gets cold."

"And when they figure bonuses," he said.

When he'd left I took an elevator up to the top floor and found the Green Room.

It took up the whole of the top floor, but it had been cut and sliced into smaller areas, cutesy little rooms, alcoves, nooks to hide in. The lights were low. Girls with less clothes than my downstairs waitress hovered here and there. A blind male pianist picked out old songs and sang them throatily and well into a microphone at a piano bar. I took a vacant high chair there and ordered another drink. A pretty waitress about half my age brought it and stood quivering until I got out my wallet.

"It's not very busy," I said. "I thought it would be."

The blind pianist cocked his head up at me and smiled.

The waitress said, "It picks up later. There's a floor show in an hour. It'll fill up then." She smiled toothily at me when I tipped her a dollar.

"Hey, you're nice." She leaned a little into me so that I could feel her warmth.

"What time do you get off from here?" I asked.

She sighed. "Not until two in the morning. Can you wait that long?" Her eyes seemed old and wise and sure I would.

"I'll come back. I've got a business meeting downstairs."

She gave me a nod that was more businesslike. "I'll wait until one in the A.M., honey. After that I'll have to look around." She nodded. "And I'm expensive."

"All right," I said.

She patted my hand and left. I waited out "Star Dust" from the piano player and left also.

CHAPTER 4

INFILTRATION

I drove to Sam's house to sleep. From there I called Jo in Bington. I wondered idly how come Sam's phone was still in service with him in jail for several months.

Jo's phone rang for a while before she answered.

"Ah," she said. "I hoped you might call. How is it over there?"

"Interesting. The girls at the hotel wear very few clothes and they come on friendly. How'd you like to spend a few days for me there?"

"For you or with you? In clothes or out?" She laughed gently. "I'm surprised at you. I thought this was true love and not just a hotel weekend."

"I'd want you fully clothed if you can restrain yourself. And not with me, but for me. Wandering around, sitting on the big porch, listening. Eating rich meals, drinking in the bars, boozing it up like you love to do." (She seldom took even one drink.)

"Golfing? Tennis?"

"If you like."

"Unescorted, of course."

"Yes. I'll be around, but you won't even know me."

There was a short silence from her end. "I've got this girl

friend," she said after a moment. "You know her. Ann Wittenberg?"

"I remember her well," I said. They worked together in administration for the university. I'd been carefully trotted
through my paces several times in front of Ann so that I could
be examined to see if my teeth were my own and my zippers
worked.

"One girl wouldn't do," she said tentatively. "But both of
us have some vacation time coming and two girls . . ."

"You're absolutely right," I said. "And Ann could watch
you and keep you from straying. All I'd want you to do is listen and watch. Don't ask questions. Don't get anyone suspicious. You'd have to promise me that."

"Sure. What are we supposed to watch for?"

"Sin, mostly. What goes on around the hotel, gambling,
drugs, anything."

"Sounds interesting. I'll call the hotel in the morning for a
double room. Leave it to me—us." She waited a moment. "If
I like it there could we maybe go back sometime after . . ."

"If our welcome's not worn out," I said.

I went to bed in my old, small room. The house grew cold,
but I managed to get to sleep. In the night I awoke once, confused, wondering where I was. After I'd figured that out I
wondered why I'd come. I reviewed in my head what was
happening in the office, contracts and wills that needed doing,
corporate meetings to attend, enough of them to drown in. I
admitted to myself that I wasn't a good "routine" lawyer. I
had no ability to retain my attention span in areas I disliked.

That spring my associate Jake Bornstein and I had gingerly
formed a partnership (of sorts) with former Circuit Judge
Steinmetz, who was unwilling to set back and draw his retirement like a good old boy. Now we had more business than we

could handle and I'd been reluctant to come to Avalon, even for a look, because I'd known Jake would not approve. But I'd come because old ghosts and almost forgotten loyalties had beckoned.

It had been a good spring and summer for the office. Having Steinmetz in the office "of counsel" had been almost like having Senator Adams, my once partner, alive again. Steinmetz told colorful and sometimes close-to-true stories almost continuously. The secretaries adored him. Even Jake had smiled now and then during the spring and summer, although he'd not smiled when I'd left for Avalon.

I counted backward. I figured I'd been involved in two dozen plus murder cases. Many of them had been routine, cases where I'd done the job, presented the evidence, cross examined the witnesses, made my impassioned final argument, and waited for the almost inevitable verdict. A few had not been routine. Sam's seemed routine enough so far. The prosecution would tell its story, Sam would tell his. A jury could pick the verdict it wanted to believe. Sam could die, but it seemed very unlikely. Passion killers seldom die. More likely he'd serve a lot of years. Many go to prison and few die these years. Those who die are usually black or poor.

I wondered if death wasn't the kinder punishment for Sam. When we'd been boys he couldn't stand being inside for long. Classes made him restless and angry, but he'd excelled at sports. A lion of a boy/man. I tried not to think of him caged for the rest of his life, but that persistent vision kept recurring until uneasy sleep claimed me again.

In the morning I drove out to see Sam's wife, Kate Hunter. I remembered where she'd lived from kid time, but still found it difficult to relocate. The entrance road to the farm had overgrown down the years and I missed it first time. When I turned around and did find it I negotiated its turns carefully, avoiding the deepest ruts. I drove the LTD on back and parked it near an old Chevy by a small farmhouse. Both Chevy and farmhouse needed paint.

An outsized teenaged boy sat on the front steps of the farmhouse and watched me. His hair was 4 A.M. black and he was a large boy, not quite as tall as Sam, but well muscled.

"You Sam's son?" I asked, sure that he was.

"Who the hell wants to know?" he asked savagely, muscles rippling. He was Sam's boy, all right.

"My name's Robak," I said disarmingly. I stopped in front of him. "I'm your cousin if you're Sam's son. I'm also a lawyer. He sent for me to come and see him."

He considered that, still angry for some reason, maybe because I was out and his father was in jail. "They whisper where I can't hear them they're going to burn my dad. Can you stop that?"

"I can give it a hell of a try." I shook my head. "They're not going to execute him."

"They say it at school."

"Who says it?"

He shook his head, not knowing and yet knowing.

"I've forgotten your first name?"

"Sam, like his," he said. "Most of the people around here call me Junior."

"Is your mother here, Junior?"

He nodded, discarding her, still wanting to probe me. "Pop used to talk some to me about being a lawyer. I guess maybe I've heard him mention your name."

"I lived in Avalon for a while when Sam was about your age and I was a year or two younger."

He inspected me for flaws because of that and finding no eye-apparent ones, said, "I'll find my mother for you."

I stood on the porch and watched squirrels play tag in an old tree. Fall birds sang songs to each other.

In a few moments Kate came out onto the porch. She'd changed very little. Her hair was now part gray, part brown, but it glistened in the sun and she was still very lovely. She was thinner than I remembered, a tall woman with huge, lost blue eyes.

"Don," she said softly. "I didn't believe it when Junior said it was you. I thought it was someone from school again on him."

"Is he having school problems?"

"Sometimes he doesn't go. They want him back. He was number three in his class."

"I see."

She took my hands and pulled me close. "Thank you for coming. Maude said she'd asked Sam if it was all right and that he'd said she could call you, but she's forgetful at times and she'd stopped mentioning it." She smiled and pulled at me. "Come inside."

Memories came to haunt me again as I followed behind her. As a boy I'd had a hopeless crush on her. She'd been two years older than me, a lifetime at my fifteen, and she'd been Sam's girl. Somehow she'd sensed what I was feeling and she'd been the proper mixture of kind and cool so that the crush had partially abated. She'd then made certain I got around other girls, talked them up to me, and me to them, until soon there'd been a girl for me, a shy girl with golden hair (now married, three grown children).

Fifteen had been a bad age for me to live through, but like

most of the passengers, I'd survived. Kate had helped. Sam
had also helped. I remembered them both being with me the
night Mom died, helping me hold on. I owed them both for
that, even though the years had diminished the debt.

Inside we went from sunlight to dark and my eyes had
trouble adjusting. I stumbled a little. The drapes were drawn
tight, perhaps to hide a world outside which had disappointed
Kate. Somewhere in the house I could hear the boy moving
around. I followed behind Kate into the kitchen. It was
lighter there.

"Would you want some coffee?"

"All right. Black, please."

I liked it better in the light. I don't like dimness, a war
thing that has remained. They used to blow their bugles at
night and then come in waves at us.

She poured me coffee with a hand that shook slightly. I
sipped it.

"How about you, Kate? What have you done with your
life?"

She shrugged. "I was mostly just Sam's wife. I worked a little in a dress shop downtown. When Sam was indicted the
woman there let me go. I guess she had to do it."

"Why would she have to do it?"

"The town doesn't like Hunters much. They've fantasized
that little bitch into something she wasn't and Sam into some
kind of cruel monster." She watched me. "Jeb Wyman's not
going to appreciate you meddling in this case."

I shrugged. "I told Sam I'd help. I made a little start yesterday. Wyman will probably have heard that by now."

"I thank you for helping, but be careful of Jeb. He's got
men working for him and men around him who work for the

hotel and in politics. He's big in politics. No one in town wants to get crosswise with him these days and that's made him used to getting his own way."

"He was spoiled when we were kids. I remember going to the games and all of those scouts from colleges being there. He knew it."

"He's worse now."

"I'd like to see him. It was his sister who got killed. He'll know things I need to know."

"He'll give you nothing," she said. "He wants Sam buried deep and dark. You'll be an interloper to him just like you were when you came here as a boy."

I watched her. "Do you care whether Jeb gets the job done on Sam, Kate? Really care?"

She hesitated a fraction. "I guess I do. Sam's always been a big kid. Maybe that's why he and Junior are so close. Sam never grew up. Maybe he has some now, but he hadn't before. He was always a man who could drink more, fight more, hunt and fish better than anyone else. I left because it was what he wanted and what both of us needed. I'd been replaced by a newer model." She smiled wryly. "I've thought about it more with him in jail. I guess I'd take him back. Maybe someday I'd forgive him. But don't hint that to him. If he comes back it's got to be because he wants to come back, not just because I'd let him and it's the easy way." She looked away from me and then back. "I could have killed her as easy as Sam. I was here at the house alone. Junior was out someplace. No one ever even asked. They picked up Sam and that was the end of it. I guess they've got him."

"Are you telling me you killed her, Kate?"

"No. I'm telling you I could have."

"How'd it get started with her? You and Sam were always so close."

"I don't know, Don. He got moody after he left the police department. He started drinking a lot more than usual, then he started staying out all night. I knew, after a while, that there was someone. I didn't know who it was, not until Jeb called me and told me. I guess Jeb wanted it stopped. Anyway, he called. So I asked Sam about her and he admitted it. I moved out of his house and out here. I was hurt. My pride was badly dented." She stopped and thought for a moment. "But that still doesn't mean I believe Sam killed that little bitch, Don. You know Sam too, Don. Both of us know he's honorable as a child in fights. I don't think he could ever kill anyone except in a fight where they were trying to kill him."

"It could be he didn't mean to kill her," I said. "He admits hitting her. You know he's very strong, Kate."

"You don't believe him?"

"Sure, but I have to figure what a jury will believe."

"I suppose so," she said. I could tell she was disappointed in me somehow. "His enemies know how strong he is also."

"What enemies do you mean?"

"When he was on the police force and had power he made the hotel people do right. He made them scramble. No girls for sale, no big money gambling, no after-hours liquor, and no drugs. It's commonly known around town that Mr. Cowles and Jeb were after him and that they got him. Then Jeb and Sam hated each other long before the time of Sheila's death. You know it. Sometimes I can play fantasy games with myself and win. I convince me that was the true reason Sam took up with Sheila—to get back at Jeb."

"Maybe it was," I said.

"No. I know it wasn't. I—we—were getting old. Sheila was Sam's way of fighting back."

"Well, I'll check what I can. Till and Maude and Sam's lawyer say that the town's pretty much against Sam. Does he have any special friends? Anyone I could look to for help?"

"Sam has lots of friends. I guess though they'd all mostly be afraid of Jeb and the hotel. Maybe you could try Sheriff Bentz. Sam got on well with him. They used to hunt together lots. But I don't know. Bentz is cautious too."

"I can try. Tell me something else. If I wanted to go someplace where Jeb Wyman would see me, where would I go?"

"The race track, from what I hear. He spends a lot of time betting the horses. When he's in town I'd suppose maybe the Elks or maybe one of the Grand Hotel bars." She shook her head. "Try one of those."

"How's Junior doing other than school?"

"He worships Sam. They were more like brothers than father and son, always picking and punching and grinning at each other. When I moved, Junior didn't want to come along, but Sam talked to him, made him go with me. After the murder he had fights at school. Now he mopes around here, fighting himself."

"Call him for me," I said. "Maybe I can give him something to check on about Sam and that night."

"What would that be?"

"Sam told me he walked across the golf course. I thought there might be some chance someone saw him. I remember when I was living here it used to be a good necking place for kids."

"And if we could find someone who saw Sam crossing the course that could help?"

"If the time was right."

She hesitated for a moment. Finally she said, "How about me asking him to check it rather than you asking him?"

"All right."

"Maybe it'll help him believe I also don't think his father killed that thing."

"Sure, Kate?"

She nodded. "I'm sure, but it's all so frustrating. They've got him and I can realize that. I didn't like Jeb when we were kids, even before Moll died. He was so smooth, so much the star athlete. He thought everyone wanted him. Once he tried to move in on me when Sam wasn't around. I stepped hard on his pride."

"I tried to move in on you too," I said, smiling, but only a little.

"You were different," she said. "You were lost in a world you didn't know, adrift in a whole new sea of strangers. You had no one. Sam tried to push you too hard, wanted you to grow up overnight." She nodded. "I was something to anchor to."

"More than that," I said.

I could almost see her calculate a decision. She needed me and she could tell I wasn't yet fully in camp. She moved near and took my hand. "Help me, Don," she whispered. Her eyes invited me. "Help Sam. Please. He and I may be done, but he still needs our help." She closed her eyes and waited patiently, perhaps wearily, to be held and kissed, a sad woman seeking something.

"That's why I came," I said stolidly, not moving. "To help you and Sam. For old times. I'd rather be spending my time in Bington. I've got a law practice that needs me to be there. I've also got a girl there I'm going to marry soon."

She took half a step backward and opened her eyes. I thought I read something in them. Relief?

"That's nice," she said, her hand falling away. "That's real nice."

I looked at my watch. "I'll be going on now."

When I left I glanced up at the upper story of the house. The boy stood at a window. He was watching me. I wondered what he'd heard, what he thought. Kate waved to me from her front door.

Success for a small town these days is sometimes measured by the number of national fast food franchises the town can attract. Avalon had about a dozen pizza, steak, chicken, roast beef, and hamburger outlets. I found a Burger King at the edge of town and ordered a Whopper (no onions) and black coffee to wash it down with. High school kids bustled around me as I waited in line, calling to each other, laughing at in-group jokes I knew nothing about. It was still warm and sunny outside so I got my food in a carry-out bag and drove another mile and entered the state park, figuring to eat there on a park bench. That way I could watch the red and yellow-brown leaves fly in the soft fall wind.

The gate was unattended at this time of year so I drove to a nearby shelter house. More kids played noontime pickup soft-ball on a rough diamond in front of the shelter house. I entered and ate my sandwich and drank my coffee. By the time I was done the kids were gone.

It was but a five-minute walk to the steps that led down to the falls. I could stand near the top of those steps and see the water pour over to splash about a hundred feet below into a turbulent pool.

Moll had died at the bottom of the right side of the falls.

Now, it looked as if there was some sort of fence at the top to protect the unwary. Then, there'd been nothing. We theorized later she must have been running through the darkness, not knowing exactly where she was, unaware of being at the edge. She'd landed far out, too far for a mere slip.

I could see the spot where we'd found her body.

It had been a family picnic planned by Judge Hunter's wife. Almost everyone had been there, all the family. There'd been food and lemonade and beer for the older men. I'd stolen some of the beer, I remembered. It had been a good picnic at first.

Then Moll had vanished and died in the darkness.

Maybe that had started the whole chain of events which had culminated with the death of Sheila Wyman. How well did I really know Sam now? I'd known him then, but the years had changed me and so they must have changed him too.

I remembered Sam had hated Jeb Wyman after that night, a hate that I'd watched fester and grow. It had been well for Jeb that he'd gone on quickly to the state university. There he'd become an all-American basketball player, the only one Avalon had ever produced. He'd become a hero to the kids who'd come after him, for Avalon was a town where children were born with a basketball in one hand. I supposed that basketball had made life and business easier for Jeb when he'd returned to Avalon, but I doubted it had ended Sam's hate.

I shook my head. I was trying to understand complex events, many of which were not completely known, some of which rested on other secret happenings. That wasn't really my job. My job was to be Sam's advocate, his lawyer. I wasn't supposed to look for reasons why he could have murdered Sheila, but instead, reasons why he could not have done it.

I looked once more down at the spot where Moll had fallen and died. She'd been a vivid girl, not really beautiful, but so full of life and spirit that she'd seemed beautiful. She'd been a year younger than Sam, a year older than me. She'd been a sometime buffer between us when I'd occasionally resisted Sam's ongoing ideas of change for me.

I missed her still.

I turned back and walked to my car.

CHAPTER 5

UNDERSTANDING THE TERRITORY

I drove to the hotel and parked in the huge lot and hiked up to the lobby.

Another desk clerk worked behind the marble counter. This one was named Matthew and he'd been eight spotless years with the hotel, if one could believe his badge.

"Matthew, my name is Robak and I'm here to see your Mr. Cowles," I said.

He nodded with either real or feigned enthusiasm. "He told me to let him know the moment you arrived." He tapped on the executive door behind the marble counter and entered while I waited.

Roger Cowles returned with him. He'd switched today to a handsome, dark-blue pinstripe. He smiled winningly at me and it was hard for me to feel he wasn't an ally.

"Nice to see you again, Mr. Robak. Please come into my office."

I found the way and followed him in. There was a huge desk. It was neatly piled with papers. I had the feeling that Roger Cowles could reach into any stack and come out with precisely the paper he sought. I admired and hated people like that.

"I talked with the prosecutor about what you wanted," he said. "He told me what I had to give you and what I didn't have to give you, but I'm not going to stay exactly within his guidelines. Again, we here at the hotel have nothing to hide in the Wyman matter. So, what would you like to see?"

"A list of the guests in the hotel that night, a list of all hotel activities for that day and night, the names of all employees who were working or present at the time Sheila Wyman was killed. That would give me a good start."

He nodded agreeably. He reached for the largest stack on top of his desk and sorted through it. "I did some checking on you, Mr. Robak. You've done a lot of criminal work, haven't you?"

"Yes. Most days I think I've done far too much of it." I took the papers he handed me. He gave me a neat manila folder to put them in.

"Start with this," he said. "I'll talk with you about any questions you have when you've looked it over. The prosecutor told me you had no right to talk to our people while they're on the job. You'll have to see them at their homes. That's fair, isn't it?"

"Of course. I don't want to interfere in your routine." I glanced at the papers he'd given me. There were neat copies of registration cards, four to a page, there was a schedule of events for August 4, more than two months back. There were also copies of employee time cards. On the short list of meetings I spied one curious thing. There was a gap in the page.

"What was here?" I asked, pointing to the gap.

"Probably a canceled meeting," he said, dismissing it. "If it was canceled late then the typist making copies of the list wouldn't bother making up a new original. She'd erase the line or blank it out with correction fluid."

Before the blank there was a 7 P.M. dinner meeting listed in the Talbot Parlor for State Southeastern Ford Dealers. After the blank there was another dinner meeting in the Presidential Room for the Six County Realtors Association for 8 P.M. I nodded and closed the manila folder. I'd want to look it over carefully, but not just now. And I knew some realtors in Bington and also the local Ford dealer. I could check the list of hotel guests to see if anyone I knew had been in attendance.

"Would the cards list all your guests who were in the hotel?"

He nodded. "I told them to go back and pick up anyone still in house on that day, whether they checked in that day or not."

"And do all your employees stamp in on a time card?"

"I don't, but everyone else does."

I hefted the manila folder. "Thank you."

"I told you we'd try to cooperate. And it was a short house. We lost a lot of money that night."

"I'm sorry you did."

"Let me show you around the hotel?"

"No. No thank you. Some other time. I know it some already from conventions I've attended here." I smiled at him carefully. "Last night was my first visit to your Green Room. I don't remember it from before."

He gave me a thoughtful look. "It's new. Gives our convention crowds a place to blow off steam and spend their money."

"It does that. What's the going rate?"

"For drinks?"

"For drinks, for dinner, for the girls."

"The first two I can tell you about. Costly. The girls I know nothing about. I'm not their keeper, only their employer."

"I see. Thanks again for this," I said, tapping the manila folder.

He nodded and then insisted on walking with me to the main door and out onto the porch. It seemed to me that many people watched us. I saw one face I knew, the golf warden I'd seen as I looked over the course after leaving Sheila's room. He nodded at me, perhaps remembering me too.

At four o'clock that afternoon, after going over the registration and time cards without finding anything startling, I walked into the Avalon Elks Club. I exhibited my membership card to the bartender and ordered a drink. I sat at the bar. The crowd was sparse and if Jeb Wyman was present he'd changed enough for me not to recognize him. Some of the other patrons looked me, the stranger, over curiously, but most ignored me.

The bartender swiftly brought my drink and refused my money. "First one for an out-of-town visitor's always on the house, Mr. Robak," he said affably, remembering my name from my membership card. He was a gnome of a man with eyes that glittered coolly behind thick glasses. High blood pressure or too much indulgence in what he purveyed had made the blood vessels in his nose prominent.

"Jeb Wyman been in?"

"Not yet. Some days he comes along about this time if he ain't at the track. You know Mr. Jeb?"

"I used to know him. I've not seen him for years. Is he still thin?"

The bartender smiled. "You ain't seen him for a lot of years

is right. He's a big man in Avalon in more ways than one."
He watched me. "You an old friend or something?"

"An acquaintance."

He shrugged, not caring. "Well if you wait he'll likely be
along. He'll want his Heineken's beer. We keep it for him
special. He'll have at least one man along with him to make
sure his world works right. That'll probably be Abner. Abner
drinks Tab. Watch that one, mister." He nodded and moved
away, leaving me alone. If I was to be trouble he wanted
nothing to do with it. I had, however, sensed a dislike of Jeb
Wyman.

The bar was dim and quiet. There was a jukebox in the
corner and one beer-drinking customer wanted to turn it on,
but was dissuaded by the bartender.

Now and then the outside door would open and I'd turn
casually, with the rest, to inspect new arrivals. Things grew
busier as it grew later.

The afternoon paper came and the bartender got it at the
door and returned to the bar looking it over, squinting in the
gloom. He handed it to me.

"Something about you here, Mr. Robak," he said.

I looked at the paper. There was a story, upper left, front
page. My picture was above it. It was an old picture that I'd
seen before in the big daily in the state capital. I turned the
paper to catch the best light. The story concerned my repre-
sentation of Sam Hunter. It had a list of other murder cases
I'd appeared in, "sensational murder cases," it said.

"Thank you," I said to the bartender, handing him back his
paper.

He nodded at me. In a while I could see him passing the
paper here and there. Eyes watched me more curiously.

As I sipped drink three I was rewarded. Jeb Wyman arrived. He was accompanied by two men. One of those two I knew from law school days: Judge Cory. The three of them sat at a table in the far corner of the room and Wyman beckoned imperiously at the bartender.

Wyman was big. When I'd known him he'd been six-six and maybe one-ninety. Now he had to be pushing two-seventy. He'd developed a prominent belly and his face was a study in jowls. Most of his hair had vanished with the years. He looked like a caricature of the Jeb Wyman I remembered from long years ago, recognizable, but bloated.

Judge Cory was a tiny man. He had a flat face and curly, dark hair, Greek maybe. He was a year or two younger than me, forty maybe. An old war had made me senior to some of my law school class in years. Cory sat next to Wyman and they spoke in low voices to each other. I saw the bartender pour Cory's drink and it was Tab, like that of the huge, sturdy young man I took to be Abner, who attended or guarded Jeb Wyman.

When the bartender delivered the tray of drinks he bent and whispered something to Judge Cory. He handed him the paper and pointed. Cory's alive, blue-black eyes came up then and caught mine. He grinned.

"Why there's my old law school buddy, Don Robak," he called. He jumped to his feet. Wyman raised a hand and re-strained him.

"Come on back here, Robak," he ordered, seemingly genial enough about it. "Bring your drink and come on." His voice was commanding.

I got up obediently and went to the table.

"Drag him up a chair, Abner," Jeb ordered.

"Thanks," I said. Abner grinned at me. He lifted up a

chair from near another table with one finger and hefted it high and sat it down.

"Shake hands with Abner Foltz," Wyman said.

Abner put his hand out, but I acted as if I'd not heard. It was a large hand and Abner seemed to me to be the kind who'd enjoy using it. He grinned some more at me when my hand stayed down.

Jeb ignored the byplay, not even looking at us. "I heard several places you were around," he said. He laughed a little. "When you first came to Avalon, years ago, your cousin Sam used to have to pull your chestnuts out of the fire for you, so I guessed maybe you'd be around trying to save his." He shook his head sorrowfully. "I'm sorry for Sam, Don. I truly am. We never got along good after high school, but we lived in the same town, and I am sorry for him."

"And I'm sorry about your little sister," I answered. "I'm taking a new look at it for Sam. He says it wasn't him who did it."

Jeb shook his head. "I sure wish that was so, but it was him all right. He never forgave or forgot. You ought to remember that. He hated me for Moll ever since that picnic. I believe Sheila was his way of getting himself even. Moll died. So Sheila had to die. Eye for eye, tooth for tooth." He looked at me. "I can remember him saying that lots when we were kids."

I remembered it also. I nodded.

"That's his way and the town out there knows it."

"So could anyone who wanted to set him up."

Jeb shrugged. "There isn't anyone else."

Judge Cory said carefully, "I really shouldn't be listening to this."

Wyman smiled coolly at Cory. "This isn't evidence, Judge. It's just a few old friends together sitting around making comments about the dead past. But you can leave if you want."

Cory shook his head wryly, but stayed seated.

"I'm going to take a good long look into it," I said again.

"Sure. That's the boy, Don. You do that for him. Help him all you can. I've heard around you do lots of criminal work and that you're supposed to be good at it. Even our local newspaper recognizes that. Sam sure needs the best." He smiled inquiringly at me. "What's he paying you with, by the way? All he's got is that old house and he owes a big mortgage on it."

"I'm not concerned," I said.

"A man should worry about things like that. I heard you were going to try marriage again. A married man can't work for nothing."

"Who told you I was getting married?" I asked, chilled just a bit.

"I find out things," he said. "I have friends. I ask questions."

I smiled at him. "Like me, maybe. Sometimes I dig around in things for the pure hell of it. You never know what you'll find until you turn over all the rocks."

He frowned, not liking my answer. "It's a peculiar time for Avalon, Don. It's a very good political time because we got us a local boy who's made good, who's going to be in the news a lot, who might be President or maybe vice-president. We area people who are backing him don't want anything coming up to blur his candidacy, any problems for him. And Avalon has got a hotel that makes a bit one year and loses it the next. We've also got a host of local people who believe that Sam killed my sweet baby sister, me among them. Do you think you can do your digging so that you help Sam and don't cause my town and my people problems?"

"I don't know, Jeb. I'm not out to hurt anyone. I knew Bratewell years back and think he's all right. And the hotel has been cooperative. My problem is that I can't promise anything. What happens happens."

"Can I help you ease it along in any way?" he asked intently.

"Undoubtedly. I repeat I don't want to cause problems. But I have to do my job."

"Your job's in the courtroom," he said reasonably.

"But also in finding out what's to be said there. I'll need to do a lot of that."

"Then you'll need to talk some with me?" he asked.

I nodded.

"How about going to the track with me, say maybe tomorrow, and we can talk some?"

"All right," I said. "Could I ask you a few more questions now?"

"Ask away," he said, smiling a little, apparently sure we'd reached some kind of gentleman's agreement.

"How come your sister worked for the hotel?"

"Where else could she work? Avalon hasn't a lot of jobs. In the course of things she applied for a job there. Roger Cowles told me that she was doing a good job for them."

"Was she dating Roger Cowles?"

He shook his head. "Not seriously. She was only serious with Sam. Roger's a bachelor. He squires lots of the pretty ladies around the hotel. He's too old to bite many of them."

"What other men was your sister going with at the time she was killed?"

"I don't know, Don. I swear it. I was against her going with

Sam, but she laughed at me. He was more than fifteen years older than she was. I'll let you in on a secret: I fought it at first, then tolerated it, and then wasn't too unhappy about it. He had her under his thumb most of the time." He shrugged. "There could have been others. She didn't tell me what she did. In fact we didn't get on that well. She was proud of me when she was a little child and I was playing college ball and then pro ball, before my knee problems. When she got older I was mostly a pain to her." He shook his head. "Sam had her under control from what I could see."

"Then why did he kill her?"

"I already said. To get back at me for Moll."

"That's unreal."

"You know it isn't. If it wasn't that then maybe they had a fight. Maybe it was an accident."

"It sounds a lot more likely than him killing her to punish you, Jeb. If he wanted to punish you he'd have come after you."

"The town doesn't think so," he said placidly.

"Maybe you've helped them think it?" I asked.

He shook his head, but I wasn't sure.

"Okay, one more question for now. Was there anything else going on at the hotel the night Sheila died? Something which somehow got canceled or marked off the activities list?"

He gave me an amused look. "Damned if I'd know. The hotel schedules and cancels things right up to the very last moment. What are you looking for?"

"I don't know. There was a blank on the schedule."

"There are blanks on most of them." He nodded and then looked me over, apparently delighted to see me. "You will come to the track tomorrow?"

"All right with me. You tell me when and where to meet you."

"We leave from the hotel. There's a bus. Be in front by eleven o'clock."

"Are you really going to try Sam's case, Don?" Judge Cory asked cautiously.

"I suppose. I think I'll need a bond hearing first, maybe some other things."

Wyman watched us, smiling a little.

"It's good seeing you," Cory said. Once, a long time back, he and I had been friends and law school classmates. We'd shared a time together. That time was now gone, but neither of us had forgotten it.

I turned back to Wyman, trying the ground further. "I ate my lunch out at the state park today."

He nodded gravely. "I go out there now and then still, trying to figure it out, understand why Moll's gone. No one but a stupid goes running around those park cliffs at night. She ran that night. She told me to come and find her." He sighed. "I never knew anyone like her. I keep remembering, after all the years, how she looked and how she was. She ruined me for other women."

I nodded. They'd been more than close. He'd had none of his arrogance with her. You could see a special thing when they were together, tell it when they touched each other. They'd been lovers. Like Kate and Sam perhaps.

"Go away for now," Jeb told me softly, not angry about it. "Seeing you reminds me of her. The town out there knows what Sam did and thinks they know why he did it. You can't save him from it, here or anywhere else. Some of my local people may even treat you bad, spit on you, because you're

here to try. You'll get half-truths and evasions, or worse than
that, nothing at all." He gave me a look that showed he had
some satisfaction in that.

"Jeb says leave now," Abner said stoutly.

"I'll do that," I said agreeably. I got up and looked down at
Jeb. I remembered he'd been a very bright student in school,
bordering on the genius level. I wondered what, if anything,
I'd gotten from him was the whole truth and thought that
maybe his remembrances of Moll might have been close.

"I'll see you in the morning," I said to Jeb. I nodded at
Cory and ignored Abner and turned away and left.

Sheriff Dell Bentz kept his office in a building next to the
ramshackle county courthouse. The jail part of the building, I
observed, seemed almost new, but the office was constructed
out of sandy, crumbling bricks similar to those that made up
the walls of the ancient courthouse. Lights mounted in front
of both buildings illuminated them. I doubted the lights had
been erected to show architectural beauty, but more probably
to keep down vandalism. Unrest grows.

It was almost seven when I parked. I went into the office. A
deputy pecked away at a typewriter, very earnest about it.
The local newspaper lay on the desk beside him. Another
deputy worked the radio. When I inquired for Sheriff Bentz
the typewriter deputy looked up and, perhaps recognizing me
from my picture in the paper, grudgingly nodded at an inner
office. I went on in.

Bentz was a big, bald man with eyebrows that jutted from
his face like flowering summer bushes. He was apparently
about Sam's age, but his face and name meant nothing to me.
I told him who I was and what I was doing there and he became cautiously friendly.

"I wasn't born here," he apologized to me. "I moved in from the next county north after I graduated high school. I was on the police with Sam and I ran for this after I got my retirement." He tapped a pencil on his desk and waited politely for me to get to the point.

"Did you or your office do any of the investigative work on Sam's case?"

He shook his head. "Local officers did it all. Usually they'll call in the state on a hot one because the state lab stuff is better. They probably used them for the skin they say they found under the girl's fingernails, but they didn't do anything else I heard about. Will Hamilton was the investigating officer and he's all right most of the time, but he has to do like he's told. Maybe they didn't ask me in because me and Sam rode together so long." He hitched at his belt. "You could try talking to Will Hamilton."

"I guess I will up the line," I said. "Have you heard anything about it since? Anything at all? Even rumors?"

He shook his head. "From what I hear the prosecutor thinks he's got a tight case. They got Sam. They can put him on the scene. They got his bloody coat and a dead girl he'd been messing with. They've got public fights. All I hear now is arguments about how long Sam will get. A few nuts even are passing the word he'll get the death penalty." He looked me over, his eyes appraising me. "If I was his lawyer and I found out Judge Cory was coming up next year for reelection and knew how tight he needs to stay with Jeb Wyman I'd think a long time before I let Cory hear it." He nodded at me. "I'll ask you not to repeat that and to forget who said it to you."

"All right."

He hesitated. I thought he was unsure of how far to trust me.

"Sam's my cousin," I said. "We go back a long, long way. Is there anything else?"

"Nothing maybe, but there's a little money which passes from the hotel to the locals." He waved a deprecating hand. "It's all fairly legal. It used to be, when I was still with the city, that we'd get a call at headquarters from the hotel and we'd get asked about providing some special guards for a convention display or something. They'd pay real good, like maybe three or four times the going hourly rate. A week's pay for a day's work. Sam never got any of it. They tried to hire him, but only at first."

"Did you get any of it, Sheriff Bentz?"

He didn't grow angry. "A little. I'm a tolerant man, Mr. Robak. I don't look for trouble, like some. I don't dislike those who do look for trouble, though. Toward the end of my time on the police I was already planning on doing this, on running for sheriff. I wasn't rocking any boats or making any extra enemies. But when Sam was in charge and told me what to do then I did it just like he said. And it was okay with me. I imagine Sam would also tell you that."

"Does Will Hamilton do any of this 'extra work' for the hotel?"

"I suppose. Will's all right. Ask him about what he does, not me."

"Exactly what kind of trouble did Sam have with the hotel?"

He shrugged. "Law troubles. Police troubles. If you've got the money and the inclination you can arrange about anything you want at the hotel. Most of us accepted that. Sam didn't. You can get drugs, hard or soft, and you can get girls or boys. You can play high stakes poker, see live lady shows and the best of the under-the-counter dirty movies. There's a big, big crap game been going on out there periodically, moving from room to room, for maybe a dozen years. You can also bet your money on the horses or on any sports event up to about any amount you want to come up with." He smiled without humor. "And it can be a tough place. Maybe five years ago now two young, smart boys from Chicago came sneaking up on them and past posted them for a wad. That's what you hear, anyway. I don't know it for sure. The rest of the rumor is that the smart boys didn't get away and if a fellow really wanted to find them he could try the river bottom." He gave me an upward look. "They've got some mean people who work in and around the hotel. Some of them sure look to me like other than hotel people, but they work there nevertheless. Do you know Jeb Wyman?"

"Yes."

"That Abner he has with him now and then is a good example. If Jeb pays him then I'll bet he gets it back some way from the Grand."

"Who owns the hotel?"

"That's a good question. My answer has to be that I don't know. Eastern money, maybe some Vegas money. It's a corporation, but I don't know of anyone local who has any stock and I've never heard of any being for sale. The board though is mostly local: Jeb Wyman, George Hamilton, who's Will's father and who runs the municipal water company, plus Roger Cowles, the manager, and the two hotshot pros, golf and tennis. There are two other people who fly in now and then when things apparently need a rough shake. I've seen them, but we ain't been introduced. The directors get big money, but I hear the amount's directly tied into what hotel profits are. Keeps everyone hopping and interested. And maybe it helps keep things loose as far as law enforcement's concerned."

"I see," I said, thinking about it. I could think of some news people I knew pretty well who'd be very interested in the hotel if they were told right.

The sheriff watched me with the cautious eyes of a politician who'd survived. "Jeb had his own particular man he backed last time I ran. I beat him out in the primary, but it was close. He says he'll probably back me for reelection next time, so you keep me out of it, hear?"

"All right."

"Somehow, when I was on the police force, every time someone was going to come down on the hotel, every time there was going to be a raid, it got leaked. The only way Sam got them to toe the line some was by doing it himself, by announcing no plans. Sure he'd take some of us, me included, along, but he never told us exactly when or what or where we were going. We'd go without a search warrant and do just what Sam ordered at the scene. That was when old Cappy was the chief and he worshiped Sam. Lawyers would scream afterwards, but Sam raided poker, arrested semi-pro ladies, confiscated betting slips, drugs, and dirty movies. He'd lose in court when it came down to that, but normally it'd get dealt. The hotel didn't like the publicity of winning. He was a pain to them, Mr. Robak."

"And now he's in jail and he lost his job."

"That's right. A bunch of us felt bad about him getting kicked down when it happened." He nodded at me. "You can only get elected to my job two times in a row. If I run and get myself elected again and if Sam would be okay then and not in jail, he could be my chief deputy. We'd have some good times. But right now, this year and until next year in November, I'm a politician. I'm not a statesman and I'm not a law enforcement officer. I'm a process server. I smile and slap people on the back. I want this job for a second term." He smiled. "They tell you around town not to mess with them people at the hotel. Maybe they're right, but I'd sure like, one time in this life, to mess with them *good.*" He sighed. "After next year."

"How about this year if you really had good reason?"

He shook his head. "No."

"Maybe something that would help Sam off the hook?"

"Have you got something like that?" he asked curiously.

"No, nothing at all. I'm just suspicious of any entity which tilts a town as much as the Grand Hotel does Avalon."

"Find something and I'll talk to you maybe," he said reluctantly. "I'm not promising a thing, but I'd talk to you." He hesitated for a moment. "I send my deputies past Till and Maude's place to watch things. I've heard Jeb don't much like that."

"Thank you for doing it."

CHAPTER 6

ALLIES ARRIVE

Outside the sheriff's office my stomach informed me it was past dinner time. The weather was pleasant enough so I walked the few blocks back to the hotel and into the lobby. Once inside I saw two familiar faces coming toward me and tried to avoid looking at them. It was Jo and her friend, Ann Wittenberg. They walked past me, ignoring me also, but laughing a little about something humorous, probably me.

It seemed peculiar to see Jo in the hotel even though I'd sent for her. She was a smallish, well made woman with a face that some people described to me as being tranquil. Alongside Ann Wittenberg, a big, stunning blonde, Jo didn't stand out at first glance. But I knew from watching other men around her and from my own experience that the longer you looked the more you liked the view. She was a very rounded woman without lumps, without angularity. When you looked at her you felt the heat. She had a finished air to her. She always seemed so apparently happy, even when she was not, that she had an aura to her. She'd become for me, in less than two years, what I was sure I wanted and what I hoped I'd soon have. In addition to being lovely she was also a complex and bright person, very facile. She could play the dutiful daughter type when I was into advice; she could mother me when I was down; she could be both lover and loved; she could give cold, cutting direction when I was overwrought or overboard. I knew she was brighter than I'd ever be, but she was pushy about it only when I needed the pushes. I thought her the most lovely, complete person I'd ever met. She had a fine job in administration with the university; she had money of her own. It made me wonder why she had accepted me.

I entered the bar I'd been in before after Jo and Ann were safely past. My last night's waitress came to my table. She smiled down at me familiarly.

"I found out about you," she said. "People were talking about you after you left last night and again today. And I saw your picture in the local paper. You weren't a friend of Sheila's, you're Sam's relative and now you're one of his lawyers. I've heard it a half dozen places. Sam's hired himself a hotshot trial lawyer." Her voice was half playful, half serious. She wore either last night's Band-Aids or a fresh issue. "You better watch yourself around this town, mister."

"Should I be careful of you?"

"Not me, but lots of people."

"Did you know Wanda Shefel too?"

"I'm not supposed to talk with you about the case, not here at work anyway. Besides that, Wanda's gone."

"Chicago?"

"I heard somewhere that's where she went." She pressed her nubile body a bit closer to my table, looked right and then left to make certain we weren't under observation. Satisfied, she dropped a tiny piece of paper in my hand."

"You want what you had last night? E.T. and water?" she asked nervously.

"Sure. That's fine."

She brought me a drink and hurried away when I tried to

slow her. I gulped the drink dry, left money plus a generous tip under the glass, and went out of the bar toward the dining room. On the way I came to the mall of shops, a men's store, a gift place, a large fashion dress shop for women, and a curio place. I tried to make sure I wasn't being watched and read the note.

It said, "See Ken. 2026 South Lanier. Nine tonight."

It was now almost eight. I decided therefore on the hotel coffee shop. I ordered a club sandwich and sat and thought while I waited for it.

I was leery of the situation. The cocktail waitress had reported my conversation last night and then passed me a note. Nine at night, at this time of year, would be full dark. If I remembered the geography of the town, Lanier in the 2000 block south would be checkerboard town, part black, part white, an area of weather-beaten homes, small, grassless yards, and the smell of poverty, cheap food, and cheap wine. A rough area, near the municipal sewer plant.

My sandwich came and I ate it without enthusiasm. I reflected that my spirit of adventure had faded with the years and that I'd grown cautious and suspicious. But my curiosity remains.

The house I sought was built shotgun style, one room behind the next, on a narrow lot. There was a small porch with two sagging lawn chairs. The sidewalk back to the porch had crumbled back to the components which had originally created it and it was covered with a thin coating of crushed leaves. I approached the house cautiously, watching both behind and in front.

I tapped on the door. Far back, at the rear of the house, I could see some light through the imperfect glass of the door.

The man who came to the door was tall and emaciated looking and he was black.

He nodded. "You Robak?"

"Yes."

"Come inside quickly. The last thing we need is someone seeing you around here. Bad enough you had to drive in and park your car somewhere." He peered out the door. "Where'd you park it?"

"A few blocks away."

"Did you maybe think to check to see if you were being followed?"

"I don't think I was, but I'm not an expert."

He looked cautiously out the door again, partially reassured. "I don't see anyone, but who knows these days." He shrugged philosophically. "You come on in."

I followed behind him once he'd unblocked the door by moving from it. He waited me past and then closed the door behind us. He led me through dim rooms to a kitchen where the blinds were drawn. He motioned me to a chair at the kitchen table and I sat, picking a chair where my back was to the wall. I looked around and waited. The kitchen stove was an old electric with two burners missing. The paint and paper were streaked and dingy. The linoleum was starting to come loose from the floor.

"I could make us some instant coffee," the black man said.

"Are you Ken?" I asked, shaking my head.

"Sure. Ken Dickson."

The name meant something to me. I thought for a moment and then remembered. "You're the one who delivered sandwiches to the room the night Sheila Wyman was murdered."

"Sure I am," he said contemptuously. "That's me, but that's not why you're here. We didn't know about you so we did

some checking. We talked to people who know you in Bington and they said you were maybe all right. They said you
wouldn't be no special friend of Bratewell's and that you
don't belong to his party."

"That's correct. Tell me first what you saw the night Sheila
Wyman was killed."

He shrugged. "Not much. I took them sandwiches. She'd
ordered them from room service. It was a good hour before
she's supposed to have died. I didn't see a thing out of the ordinary. Mr. Hunter came to the door and took them from me
and gave me a two-buck tip." He smiled. "Probably her
money. She seemed to have plenty of it. Once I heard a
rumor around the hotel she was selling for the right price and
to the right people."

"A prostitute?"

"Not all the time, but she sure lived good for what she
made."

"What else did you hear?"

He shook his head. "Not anything else on her."

"Then what is it you know about Bratewell?"

"She gets in that, too," he said. He smiled. His teeth were
peculiar. They looked as if they'd been filed down. A lot of
gum showed and the teeth were sharp, almost feral. Other
than that and his extreme thinness he seemed ordinary
enough.

"I belong to a small political group. We don't like Bratewell and don't favor him as a candidate. We thought maybe
you could help us when we told you some things."

"What sort of things?"

"For a starter the good Senator knew Sheila Wyman."

"I'd be surprised if he didn't. Her brother's knee-deep in
politics and he's Bratewell's man."

"There's some evidence Bratewell knew her real well, knew her in the biblical sense."

"What evidence?"

"Nothing real good. No eye witnesses to them being caught in bed. The thing is there are other people who feel like me who work at the hotel. The Senator's always very discreet, very careful. When he wants something he don't just go get it, he sends someone to fetch it. I've seen that happening. I've also seen Sheila coming and going from his rooms at the hotel. That big man, Abner, he did the delivery."

"Did Abner stay?"

He nodded reluctantly.

"In the old wing?"

He shook his head. "No. Where Bratewell keeps his suite. In the new part near the domed pool."

"I didn't know he kept a suite," I said. I'd looked over the registration cards and had not seen his name as a registered guest. But I also remembered seeing the "Bratewell for President" sign. There had been rooms registered that way.

"Big shots come to visit him at the hotel, he puts them up if need be. When he's not in residence then some of his people use the rooms, but he sneaks in and out of them. He's got his headquarters sign above the porch. You've seen it."

I nodded and thought for a moment. "What you're really telling me is that Sheila Wyman occasionally visited those rooms. That's all you have?"

He smiled. "It's something for you. It's enough to get him in the courthouse door. They tell around that you're a mean lawyer."

"Who tells?"

"That's what we've heard. We don't care and you shouldn't care whether Bratewell was messing with her or one of his people was with her. She was there inside his rooms and now she's dead. All you've got to do is ask me the right questions at a trial or hearing. No matter how it turns out it won't help Bratewell."

"I see."

"I'm going to tell you something else you ought to know. I got asked to a secret meeting recently. It was old hotel people, men and women who'd worked in the hotel for a long time. They think I'm right in with them. It was a hot meeting with a lot of names being called. The final thing was we all took a solemn oath that if we wound up on Sam's jury he'd get found guilty if it could be worked."

"How many people at the meeting?"

"Twenty or so. All people who've worked a long time at the hotel."

"Can you get me the names?"

"I can probably remember most of them if need be. You get to ask jurors questions, don't you?"

"Yes."

"Then be careful and suspicious of anyone who's been working for the hotel long or who has someone in their family who's worked there awhile."

"Who ran the meeting?"

"Link Ellison. He's the head bellman and Roger Cowles's number one flunky." He nodded at me. "I've even got some more for you. This is gossip, but I think if you went to the courthouse and checked the deed records for land near the hotel you might find something interesting. I've heard around some of it belongs to Jeb Wyman and Roger Cowles. They might be blinds for or in partnership with Senator Bratewell."

"It's legal to own land," I said. "Does the adjoining land have some particular value?"

"It will if they get their casino law through the legislature."

He must have seen my face.

"You didn't know about that? They're going to try to get one through next session, try real hard. After Atlantic City there's a good chance they'll get the job done. It would be county option, but I hear they believe this county would jump for it. There's supposed to be a lot of money around to buy it if need be."

"And Bratewell's into that?"

"His people are. That's enough to sink him along with the other stuff I've given you."

"Just exactly what is this political group you belong to?" I asked curiously.

"Nothing you'd ever have heard of—it isn't like that. It isn't basically violent or subversive, not yet anyway."

"What is it then?"

"A lot of thinking black and white people decided, way back the line when Bratewell was governor, that he was a big step backward. He's not for blacks, he's not for the poor, he's against unions and most social programs. Our problem with him is that he talks pretty good about how he believes—he persuades a lot of people he's right. He's pretty and he looks good on television. While he's one of many candidates he's vulnerable to the things he's been into here in Avalon. Should he become the one, single candidate for his party, he's no longer vulnerable in the same way. His imperfections will get lost in larger issues." He nodded at me, very intent about it. "So we're trying hard to sting him before he gets to the top of the heap." He watched me. "Will you help us?"

"I'll look around," I said. "Maybe."

"What you mean is if it suits your purpose then you'll help us?"

"If it suits Sam's purpose," I corrected.

"Then understand that if we see another chance to do a number on Bratewell we'll do it without even thinking of your client. We'll use our weapons where we think they'll do us the most good. The best way to use this one, we figured, was where you subpoenaed him as a witness in a hearing or trial and the sooner the better. The news people would pick that up like hound dogs on a summer hunt. But if we don't know . . ."

I owed Bratewell nothing. I was seeing the first offer of help I'd really had since I'd come to Avalon.

"I might promise to subpoena him for the bond hearing if one's held up the line," I temporized.

"Are you going to have a bond hearing?"

"I think so."

"We'd hold off doing anything if you did promise."

"I can't promise anything," I said. "But my inclination right now is to press for a bond hearing."

He nodded, satisfied a bit. "If they get wind of what you're doing someone could get real worried, someone for Bratewell, someone for the hotel. You might wind up in the river." He smiled, amused about that.

"Let's hope not," I said, but it was something to worry on. I looked around the kitchen, seeing again the old, half-working stove, the cracked linoleum, the stained walls. "Do you live here?"

"Not me," he said, smiling more broadly. "I graduated *cum laude* from a big, fancy university fifteen years back, Mr. Robak. Someone with a background like that couldn't live in a dump like this and wait tables for a living, now could they?"

"I don't know," I said. It becomes easier to take up causes

as the world disintegrates and I didn't need his cause just now.

"Tell me more about this casino law?" I asked.

"All I know is that they think they can get it done. I served Mr. Wyman and Mr. Cowles one night in the dining room. Mr. Wyman had been drinking some and he was talking about it. I can stay real close to a table without even being noticed." He smiled bitterly. "Mr. Wyman, he was confident."

"Thank you for talking to me," I said. If they were going after a casino law and had known it and planned it for a long time, then perhaps Sam's story had more merit. An ex-policeman sitting outside and heckling them in the area newspapers could be an embarrassment for them, a liability. It seemed to me, thinking about it, that they'd then have killed Sam, dropped him in the river, or perhaps tried to make his death look accidental, rather than try to implicate him in a murder. And would they have murdered the chief conspirator's sister on hotel grounds? I remembered what Till had said about the men who'd tried to hurt/kill Sam. Perhaps there was more than a single group, more than one planner.

I knew Bratewell. I'd spent two years in his legislature. I remembered him as a quiet, correct man, then not one of the night runners, then not a woman chaser. The opportunities had been almost limitless for that sort of action in those tumultuous days. But I'd not heard a word about Bratewell and knew I would have. Had he changed that much since? I'd heard vaguely that his wife was ill, a chronic illness which took her from his side much of the time. Was it possible he'd taken up a new hobby?

"I'm going to move on now," Ken said. "You should leave with me. I told my people they could have their house back by about ten o'clock." He looked at a cheap watch on his left arm. "It's not that time yet, but I'll want you to leave with me." He smiled. "It truly isn't my house."

"All right," I said.

We parted at the front door. He faded down the porch and into side-yard shadows. I walked out the disintegrating walk and got into my LTD two blocks away. I took another look around, but saw no one.

I was curious about the house.

I started up and drove another block. There was no traffic to be wary of. I stopped and pulled the LTD into a spot away from the nearest streetlight. I walked back to a place where I could watch the house I'd just left.

No one came for a long time. I stood under a tree and smelled the odor of the falling leaves. I listened to the night sounds of the neighborhood, someone loudly playing disco records, a small, wild scream and then laughter from a house a few doors away. I was uncomfortable standing and watching, spying on the neighborhood, but I waited.

My watch was finally rewarded. An old car chugged up and two people got out after it was parked. One of them was my cocktail waitress, the other, a heavy, bearded young man with a thin, beaked nose. They went inside the house. I edged over into the yard and tried to listen at a window. I could hear voices inside, but insufficiently to make out what the conversation concerned. Once I thought I heard my name, but that could have been imagination or paranoia.

After a while the lights went out and the house was silent.

I walked again to the LTD and drove to Sam's house. I parked behind it in the shed. I found the small key Till had given me and locked the shed door behind me. It was deep dark. Through the gangway between the houses I could see light. I walked to the front.

Aunt Till sat on the long porch. There was no sign of Maude, just Till rocking in her chair, slowly moving, humming a hymn to herself. "Rock of Ages."

"Hello, Aunt Till," I called.

She started a little and then nodded, not really seeing me in the darkness at the edge of the porch. She peered out into the night.

"What time is it?" she asked.

"After ten."

"That late," she said, dismayed about it.

I remembered something. "Aunt Till, where can I find Major Potts?"

She shook her head, angry at my question. "What could you possibly want with that drunken old windbag?"

"I'd like to see him. I remember him from the time I lived here in Avalon. Don't you remember? I used to cut his grass and fire his furnace."

"You used to cut our grass, too."

I smiled. I had cut their grass. I'd always had to collect from Maude. Till never paid.

"I'd forget him now if I was you." She sighed, seeing I was adamant. "He's supposed to be in a nursing home in Haddaville, ten miles north on County Three-fifty. I heard a few months back he was like to die. Maybe he has by now."

"Thanks," I said. I watched her curiously, wondering why she was still out. She frowned out into the dark.

"Some bad boys came running past here a while ago. They threw rotten fruit on the porch. I cleaned it a little, but I'm feeling kind of poorly tonight. Tomorrow Maude and I'll have to scrub on some spots."

"Boys? How old were they?"

"I don't know. Big boys. They ran past screaming, 'Sam,

Sam, the hammer-hand man.' Then they threw things up on our porch. Probably bad boys from the city park. They hang around over there and smoke and drink and yell things at passing cars. Sam used to run them off."

"If they come past again save what they throw and I'll deliver it back where it might be coming from."

She shook her head. "Now, where would that be?"

"I'll find out."

"You always were a mean one. Just like Sam." She sighed and tried to get up, but then sat back into her chair. "I'm going in soon. The phone in Sam's has been ringing some."

"Would you want me to help you in?"

"No. I'll stay out just a little longer. The weather's still fine. It won't last this way much longer. Maybe I'll nap out here." She shook her head. "No. Maude would come out for me if I tried that."

I went over and sat on Sam's smaller porch and thought for a time, while I watched her. She dozed fitfully in her chair. The night wind was warm enough and she had her long shawl on.

After a while Sam's phone began to ring.

I went inside and answered.

It was Jo. She said, "I've been trying to call you."

"I hope you're not using your room phone."

"Secret operatives are smarter than that. There are pay phones in the lobby. I'm in one of them. We got checked in early this afternoon. I saw you in the lobby and I know you saw Ann and me. So I thought I'd give you a call.

"Thanks," I said, knowing there was more. I waited.

"You never ask questions of me, do you?" she said.

"No. There's no reason."

"You ask them of other people."

"Ah, but they don't like to talk."

"All right, all right. We spent most of the late afternoon on the big front porch. Two gentlemen from Indianapolis tried hard to pick us up and make us a working part of their festive Midwest convention of savings-and-loan executives. We got to hear a lot of gossip about the hotel."

"Like what?"

"You want to bet a horse, there's a room in the basement where you can make a bet. You have to get okayed by someone, but that's apparently no big problem. One of the Indianapolis men said there's a big poker game tonight, but he's not into it, doesn't know exactly where it's at or anything. He just casually knows another guy who comes to play in it, a pro gambler, and he saw him around yesterday. Some remarks were made, when we weren't enthusiastically cooperative about being picked up, that there were plenty of fish available in the Grand Hotel sea." She was silent for a moment. "Gee, those waitresses don't hardly wear a thing. We went for an after-dinner drink in the Green Room. You could smell the pot." She laughed her tinkling laugh. "I had two more offers there."

"You promised to save yourself for me," I said, smiling only a little.

"Where and when?" she asked, still laughing a little. "All I get are promises."

"Soon," I said.

She continued: "One of the offers was to go along to see a porno movie, for starters. And what's a snuff movie, Don?"

"One where a participant apparently gets killed. Most of them are faked things. I've heard a few of them aren't. It's the new 'in' thing for screwball deviates."

"This one guy I was talking to said he'd heard movies like that got made in the hotel."

A tiny alarm bell went off back in my head. It rang for a long moment and then fell silent as reason returned. *Surely not Sheila Wyman?*

"One could be made about anyplace you could find willing participants." *Like the Grand Hotel.*

"It looked to me like there were lots of possible candidates in that Green Room. That place was almost too much to believe, Don."

"I know. I was in there last night."

"What for?"

"Checking it, seeing it. Looking over the territory. You're a sweet country girl and that's why it shocked you," I said.

"I'm not and you, of all people, very well know it," she sniffed. "But I never saw entertainment that raw in a first-class hotel. Of course it was mostly men, stag men, watching in there. And the show girls didn't do that much, they just made it look like they were doing lots, to men, to each other. The lights were real low. The guy who took me in tried to grab me and I spilled my drink on him."

I was beginning to get second thoughts about having her in the hotel.

"He's kind of cute, though," she added wickedly. "I mean, if you like the type."

"Tell me what type and I'll try to change."

"Lose your hair, put on weight, and smoke a stinky cigar, for starters," she said.

I asked, "Anything else?"

"If you said, 'pretty please,' I could sneak out and meet you," she said softly. "You could pick me up out by the parking lot and bring me back later?"

I was tempted. They might know my car by now, but no one seemed to be following me.

"Half an hour?" I asked.

"Yes," she said. "Far end of the parking lot right where the drive starts in towards the hotel."

We said a temporary good-bye.

CHAPTER 7

THREATS

I called Steinmetz long distance in Bington. He was a perpetual insomniac, his active brain working twenty plus hours out of every twenty-four. Seventy plus and still going strong.

"Steinmetz here," he said robustly, answering in the middle of the first ring.

"Bully for you. This is wandering Robak."

"It would have to be. No one else would use the word 'bully.' You're very warm in what you're doing over there in Avalon. Harv, at the bank, told me they'd had calls about you. A political friend of mine called me and said they'd had an inquiry. Then our mayor stopped me on my way to what my doctor laughingly calls lunch and wanted to know what you were doing messing around over in Avalon. One more thing, and this might be important: According to the local police someone broke into your apartment last night. At least he had a report where one of Bington's finest found your back door broken open and thought things had been rummaged through. They'd like you to check and call them if you find anything missing. That's when you return from foreign wars."

"All right," I said. The idea of someone prowling through my apartment gave me a momentary feeling of sickness.

What was there was mine, my private world. I could think of nothing worth much in the apartment. Maybe the television or my new blender?

"With all the interest and phone calls and the burglary I thought maybe someone might be looking for an edge," Steinmetz said.

"That's possible. The U. S. Senator seems to be vaguely involved. Before my stint here is completed I could get even warmer. I'm helping my cousin, who's in deep trouble and charged with murder. Some of the locals don't like that." I dug around in the file I'd gotten at the hotel. "Can I get you to check something for me in the morning?"

"Why not. All I've got are half a dozen wills to write, a complicated divorce settlement to work out, plus I've got to start getting ready for the Treat damage case, unless we're going to ask for *another* continuance."

"Not yet," I said.

"Do you mean don't ask for a continuance yet or don't figure on trying it yet?"

"Don't ask for a continuance yet."

"Tell me what it is you need."

I gave him the date Sheila had died. "On that day there were several meetings at the Grand Hotel. People from our area were probably in attendance. One of them was for real estate people, the other for Ford dealers. None of our locals checked into the Grand Hotel, but it's close enough to drive back and forth from Bington. Call around and see if anyone was here that night. See if anyone remembers anything else going on about the time of their meetings, what they saw and heard in the hotel that day. Anything at all might help. Can you do that?"

"Will try," he said. "Anything else?"

"If you get the chance with anyone else inquiring for me you might tell them I'm in Avalon on a hot trail. You could tell them how dogged and mean I am."

"Lie for you, you mean? You want me to lie?"

I smiled at the phone. "It should come easily to a retired judge."

I left him sputtering for once when I hung up.

I used the back door in case Aunt Till was still on her porch.

I took Jo back to the Grand about two in the morning. I drove her boldly up to the steps. No one was in view. I let her out and watched her until she'd climbed safely up to the second-story porch.

I returned to my small room and undressed. The night air had cleared my head and the house seemed full of odors that my nose couldn't identify, odors I didn't remember smelling before. I knew nothing about the heat for Sam's house so I endured the cold as best I could, hunched into a ball in the small bed, trying to remember Jo and her warmth.

The phone rang again about four in the morning. I got up from a half sleep and ran shivering to answer it, thinking it was Jo or Judge Steinmetz.

The voice was harsh, partially muffled: "Get out or die," it said.

"Huh? This is the Jones residence," I replied.

"How's that?"

"Jones residence. Who did you want at this time of the morning?"

The phone slammed down. I rehung and sat and waited expectantly. In a few moments the phone rang again.

I answered, "Jones residence. Who's calling please?"

I got a muffled growl. "It ain't no Jones residence. Get out of Avalon or die, Robak. No more warnings for you." The phone whammed down again.

I stood looking at the buzzing receiver for a moment and then hung it up. The voice had meant nothing to me, but I was interested in the fact it had been muffled. Whoever had called thought I might recognize it now or in the future.

One odor I'd smelled earlier seemed more apparent near the phone. It smelled like smoke. I wandered around the house, leaving the lights off, blundering into things a bit. There was nothing.

I found the door down to the basement where I remembered it. Down there, long years back, I'd sometimes hidden from the world and from Sam. I risked a light and went on down. The floor was rough concrete. A gas furnace stood in one corner of the huge, single room, a washer and dryer in the other. There was a place in the upper wall where once, long ago, coal had been unloaded through a chute. I found my "fire" there.

Someone, perhaps some kid, had taken a large wad of newspapers, lit them, and shoved them through the coal chute. They'd smoldered away to almost nothingness on the concrete and they were now cold to the touch.

There was a latch inside the coal-chute door. I secured it tightly. I looked around some more, but there was nothing else. The door that led up to the outside was locked and bolted.

I went back upstairs. I found an extra blanket in a closet and tried the bed again. I was tired. I slept, warm enough now, until almost eight, late for me.

After a breakfast of swirled, fresh orange juice and black coffee plus an English muffin at one of the edge-of-town eateries, I drove around for a while. I soon found I'd acquired a follower. He was a man in an anonymous, fairly new black Chevrolet. He stayed doggedly with me, turning where I turned, speeding up when I increased speed. He was either inept as a shadower or wanted to be obvious about it. I therefore parked the LTD on the square, walked in the north door of the courthouse, and kept on going straight out the south door. I crossed a traffic-busy street, entered an alley and went half a block, then turned into the cross alley. In moments I was on Walnut Street. There, as I exited the alley, I drew the suspicious stares of a traffic policeman who was opening parking meters and pouring coins into a wheeled, steel carrier.

"Avoiding creditors," I explained, smiling a lot.

He nodded and smiled in return, probably thinking he knew me.

I walked down Walnut to Main Street. The morning was fine and I had two hours or so before I was due to meet Jeb and take a trip with him to the track.

Aunt Till's porch was vacant. It must be oatmeal time inside for her and Maude.

Two blocks past their house I recognized the Wyman house, huge and old, constructed of brick and stone, with gables and fancywork. It was a survivor of Avalon's Victorian age. There was a new Cadillac parked in the drive. I thought maybe it was Jeb's car.

I didn't want to stop while he was home.

People could be looking out windows. I might be seen and wondered about and reported if I stood long watching the Wyman driveway. I therefore turned half a block above the Wyman house and circled a couple of blocks, stepping my way through the leaves. I was a man out for a morning stroll, still noticeable, a Ray Bradbury pedestrian. People trust run-

ners these days, but not walkers, but I walked briskly so as
not to alarm anyone unduly. Now and then the sun hid
behind a cloud and made me wish again I'd brought my top-
coat with me from Bington.

When I rounded the far corner and came into sight of the
house again the Cadillac was gone. I entered the black iron
front gate and tapped brusquely on the heavy front door.
When no one answered I beat on it more strongly.

I vaguely recalled the old lady who opened the door. I'd
never known her well. Jeb's mother, Sheila's mother.

She was a small woman who wore a lavender dress with a
cameo brooch to hold it together at the neck. The dress was
old and ugly, but her hands were clean. Her hair was white
and wild, as if she'd started to comb it out and then given it
up.

"We need nothing," she murmured. Her eyes looked long-
ingly behind me at the leaves and the adjacent yards and then
up at the sun, not really seeing me.

"I'm not selling anything, Mrs. Wyman. My name's
Robak. A long time ago I used to live nearby in the neigh-
borhood. I'm a lawyer now and I'm here representing Sam
Hunter."

Her mouth made an "O" and she watched me carefully.

"I wanted to talk to you about Sheila's death and about her
relationship with Sam."

"I don't know anything about Sam. He left his wife. Now
he's in jail. And Jeb said I wasn't to discuss Sheila." She nodded. "I asked my doctor and he said it was all right to talk
about it and think about it, but Jeb says it upsets me. Maybe
he's right. He always acts like he's right." She looked up at
me. "I don't know anything anyway. Only that she was dead
and Jeb said she was bad. She had nice boyfriends when she

was growing up, but Jeb ran most of them off. When she got away from him she made other friends. That's why she was going to move from the house on the same day . . ."

"She was going to move from the house the day she died?" I asked.

She nodded. "With that big policeman. Jeb made her move more than me." A large tear came into the corner of her right eye, gathered, then rolled down her cheek. The left eye curiously stayed dry. "I didn't care what she did. She was so pretty when she was little. She came late; I was forty-six. I didn't mean for her to happen. She was a sweet child and then one day, when she was about fifteen, she grew up. Later she had some money she inherited from the trust my husband set up and then she got that job at the hotel. She still stayed here, but I saw her very little. Till and Maude told me things, told me first about Sam." She shook her small white head primly. "They didn't like it. But men were always around her. Some would come to pick her up here."

"Did Sam come here?"

"He never came here. He and Jeb hated each other. Other men."

"Did you know any of them?"

She shook her head vaguely. "Years ago I used to know them. Boys from Avalon. Then I stopped knowing them. Big men. Old men and young ones. Out-of-towners. They'd come in flashy cars. A lot of men."

"And that was shortly before she moved out?"

She nodded. "I never should have let Jeb do that to her. She wasn't bringing them in and sleeping with them here." She nodded. "I think maybe what happened is that she fought with your cousin Sam about the other men."

I gave her a half-startled look. "You know Sam's my cousin?"

She reached out and gave my hand a birdlike pat. She was an aging lady, lost in the tangled paths of her life, hopelessly trapped, maybe not completely rational, but she seemed able to function in what remained of the ruins.

"I remember you a little. And Jeb said this morning I should look out for you and not talk to you if you dared come here. But no one comes by to talk with me anymore since Sheila died." The tear appeared in her right eye again. "And I don't want or need to hate Till and Maude no matter what Jeb thinks about what the town should do." She shook her head. "I'm not allowed to go visit there. He said if I tried he'd put me in a nursing home." She reached out and captured my hand. "He's hated them since Moll died and Till ordered him off their porch. Jeb hates people real good."

"If I asked you to come into court and tell again what you've said to me would you do it?"

She shook her head violently, frightened. "He'd put me in a nursing home for sure."

"Don't you have your own money?"

She nodded. "It's my house, too."

"If he tried to do that after you'd testified, the judge would see why he was doing it. And you could hire a lawyer to represent you."

"Would you represent me?"

"If you wanted."

She shook her head, more slowly now.

"What if a sheriff came and delivered you a subpoena?"

Her eyes sparkled a little and I could see that once she'd been lovely. "You mean he'd drive into our driveway, park his patrol car, and knock on this door?"

"Yes."

"Jeb would surely die," she said, with malice in her words. She smiled conspiratorially at me. "Maybe I'd come if it happened that way. I guess I would." She nodded to herself. "Would you want to come in for coffee and talk more on it?" She shook her head to answer her own questions. "No, best not. There's someone in the neighborhood who watches me, watches this house, and calls Jeb if anyone comes. I don't know it for certain. Jeb had the house phone removed. So perhaps you'd better move on now. You can come back some other time. This time of day's real good."

"All right," I said, already backing away. We smiled at each other one more time.

"Tell Till and Maude I don't hate them even if Jeb wants me to," she called when I'd reached the sidewalk.

I nodded and turned away. I heard her shut the massive door. I walked briskly toward town.

Aunt Till and Aunt Maude were now out on their jointly owned porch washing the walls. I waved at them. Aunt Till beckoned to me. She seemed better and stronger today.

"I'm late," I called, lying a little. I walked on, making a small declaration of independence from her.

I went in the courthouse and then on up the broad, worn steps to the second floor. There I located the judge's office. A middle-aged receptionist frowned at me.

"I'd like to see Judge Cory," I said.

"Why? For what reason?"

"My name's Robak. I'm a lawyer from Bington. He'll know what it's about."

She frowned some more. "I'll see if he has any time to talk with you," she said loftily.

She left me and entered an inner office. In a few moments

she was back. This time she had a smile. I'd passed inspection.

"Judge Cory will see you."

I followed behind her. Cory was wearing a black robe. His desk was heaped high with papers. An advance sheet for the state case-reporter system lay open in front of him, turned face down now to hold his page.

"I've interrupted you," I said apologetically.

He shook his head. "No, Don boy. Just keeping up." He came around his desk and shook my hand vigorously and then thumped me hard on my shoulder.

"Old Robak," he said, thumping me some more.

I thought about thumping him a little in return, but decided against it.

"It's good to see you again," I said simply.

He motioned me to a wood chair. I sat down and he went behind his desk. On the wall behind it he had his certificates from when he'd been admitted in the state and federal courts and his certificate of election. They were all elegantly framed. He got out a cigar, clipped it precisely, and lit up, blowing acrid smoke at me.

"Did you come in here to formally get in the Hunter case?" he asked easily.

"Yes. I suppose I'm in it. More important than that, I keep getting advised here and there to take you out of it. A change of judge." I watched him for a reaction, but could read none. "Should I do that?"

He smiled coolly. "Maybe. Probably." He nodded to himself, not angry. "I'd be damned happy to be out of it, Don. You file for your change and I'll grant it so quickly your old, graying head will spin." He shook his head. "Sam's a dead bird, but I'd certainly appreciate not having to preside over his final rites." He looked me over. "Want me to get my girl to type up the motion?"

"All right," I said.

He pushed a button on his intercom and gave terse directions and then we went back to watching each other.

"Tell me about being judge. I remember, in law school, you said once it was something you didn't fancy."

He shrugged. "Everyone has to do something. I've found I can do this."

"Between us chums, is Jeb Wyman pressuring you on this case?"

He hesitated. I could almost see him rehearsing his answer. I was an old friend, but I was from another time in his life. Yet I couldn't be treated as merely an interloper. I'd used his notes in law school to study and he'd used mine. We'd studied for the bar examination together, bouncing questions off each other, sharing answers and beliefs. We'd drunk and chased women and spent our spare time with each other. He'd liked me then and I thought he still liked me now.

"You won't say anything?" he asked, anxious for the first time in our conversation. "I mean that what I say stays here and doesn't get repeated by you?"

I nodded gravely.

"Jeb wants your Sam Hunter bad. I know that to be a fact. He's hated him and been afraid of him for a long time. He was like a wild man when his sister was killed. He told the mayor what to do and the mayor then told the police chief ...d got it passed on down." He nodded. "But Sam killed her."

"He says he didn't."

"They all say that, Don." He watched me. "Do you remember who told me about this town, about Avalon?"

"No. I knew you were here is all."

"You told me. There was a note on the bulletin board at law school. I'd missed it, but you saw it and told me. So I came here and now I'm judge." He stopped for a moment and looked out his window. "The thing that makes it easy for me to tell you about Sam and Jeb is that Jeb don't give a damn about me. When I ran I had primary opposition and Jeb openly backed my opponent because he was Avalon-born. That's what he said, anyway. The real reason was he could tell him what to do better than me. So I don't owe Jeb a thing, but next year's election again. If I act too independent maybe he could look around for someone to run against me. If he gave an opponent enough money, bought them enough newspaper advertising and enough radio time, and got out the regulars he could maybe beat me. I kind of dread going back out into the world, having to start all over after six years on the bench." He shook his head. "I'm not bad at this, Don."

"You were always a good student of the law," I said. "Hell, you got me through law school. I'm sure you're a good judge."

He ignored the compliment. "Your coming here has upset Jeb. Better watch him and be careful of him. The truth's not in him. He doesn't like things that get in his way. He'll smile at you and shake your hand and put a knife in your back all at the same time." He nodded seriously.

I nodded back. "If Sam does get out and finds Jeb engineered him being in, he could make Jeb hard to catch. He'd walk right over the top of that big-handed choirboy I saw you and Jeb with."

Judge Cory grinned. "He'd do that. Sam could take 'Li'l Abner.'"

"'Li'l Abner'?"

"That's his nickname. He's a mean one. Watch him, too. I

saw Jeb give him the nod the other night. It was a good thing
you didn't shake hands with him. He likes to mangle things."

"I keep finding things which point me to Senator Bratewell."

His eyes fell and his manner became cautious. "What is it
you hear about Bratewell?"

"Just his name where I oughtn't hear it, that he and Sheila
Wyman may have been close, that he keeps rooms at the
hotel which don't show up on their guest list in his name,
that he met with her there. A few other things, that there's a
casino law in the wings at the legislature and, of course, I
hear all over he's running for President." I waited for a moment to give him a chance to digest what I'd said. "Has he
any chance at all?"

"I don't know. It's my party, but I hear very little sitting up
here. I'd guess he hasn't a prayer, but he very obviously
thinks he does. He's got some funding and he's got national
television following him around. People here in Avalon believe in him. He hasn't been much of a force in the U. S.
Senate, but then he hasn't tried to be. Maybe he's what we
need for times like these."

"He was all right when he was governor," I said.

"He's all right now, far as I know."

"The question is whether or not he was one of Sheila
Wyman's admirers?"

"The whole thing's pretty unthinkable, Don. The man's a
professional politician who has survived. He's been a member
of the general assembly, a state senator, governor, and now
he's U. S. Senator. He doesn't know anything other than politics and, as a result, he does know what happens to politicians
who chase young stuff. I don't think, like I said, that he has
much of a shot at what he wants now, but something will

wash off onto him, something will come in trade for whatever delegates he musters." He nodded at me, worry in his eyes. "Best place for me to be is out of this whole thing." He smiled gratefully at me. "Safer for sure."

The receptionist tapped on the door. She was smiling now. Perhaps it was something they'd discussed and she knew Cory was getting himself out of a problem. She handed him a sheaf of papers which he then handed to me.

"Prosecutor's outside," she said.

Judge Cory nodded. He was anxiously watching me look over the petition for change of judge and the order. They seemed okay. I signed them and handed them to him and he smiled again.

"You want to meet our prosecutor?"

"I'll have to sooner or later," I said.

Cory nodded at his receptionist. "Have Huff come on in."

The man who entered was old, late sixties, perhaps early seventies. He had gray hair and freckles that increasing age had turned to splotches.

"This is Huffman Price, our prosecutor," Cory mumbled. "Meet Don Robak who'll be representing Sam Hunter, Huff."

The man nodded at me, his eyes narrow. "I've heard some interesting things about you. I was expecting something breathing fire and with maybe nine heads." He nodded again. "So you're going to be representing Sad Sam?"

"Yes."

"Well, I'm going after all I can get."

"Don just now filed with the court a motion for a change of judge," Cory said. "I granted it."

"That'll mess up our trial date," the prosecutor said grumblingly.

"What a shame," I said.

"Look, mister—this case is going to move whether you like it or not. I'm going to resist every delay, every continuance."

"Your defendant's in jail," I said, not believing him.

"Makes no difference. I'm ready for trial."

"I'm not. It's Sam's problem and not yours if things get delayed. I need discovery, I need to take depositions, and I'll want to talk to some of the witnesses, maybe all of them. I'd imagine a bond hearing would be more in order than an early trial."

He shook his head. "No need. My file's open to you." He smiled at me, suddenly ingratiating. "We have a solid case."

"You've got a circumstantial case. Everything stopped when you had Sam Hunter in jail. I keep looking at it and wondering why that happened. Sam says he's innocent, for whatever that means in your town, Mr. Price."

"They all say they're innocent," he said with irritation.

"Some are. My client spent a lot of years as an officer on your local police force. It appears he made some enemies there. He was against sin and that was bad for your town's largest industry."

"I do believe you're being sarcastic with me, Mr. Robak." He shook his head. "Your cousin's been indicted for murder. I respect good policemen and I've got every intention of trying Sam as a bad one—and soon."

"You mean because that's the way they want it?"

"Let's say because I want it that way." He watched me, his eyes calculating. "If I could get it all together would you have your bond hearing say next week?"

His pushing was beginning to get me, anger me. If I was going to be pushed I'd push back.

"We don't even have a special judge yet," I said, trying to sound reluctant.

"We could accomplish that now. Judge Cory can name a list of three and maybe we can agree on one out of the list and show a striking of the other two." He nodded at me, his old eyes unable to hide eagerness. "How about it?"

"I might be willing to do that for a trade. What I'd want in trade are some blank subpoenas signed by your clerk so I can serve whomever I need to serve for your hurry-up bond hearing."

"Blank subpoenas?" he asked.

"About a dozen of them. Some of them I'll want to serve myself and others I'll get your sheriff to serve as necessary and as we proceed."

He mulled it over, now doubtful of me. There had to be pressure on him to get the case moving, keep it going forward.

"All right," he said. "I'll go down and get them for you from the clerk's office while Judge Cory's Abbie is typing the papers. Who are you going to name, Judge?"

Cory gave us the names of three judges from surrounding jurisdictions. I knew two of them and thought either of the two would be all right.

"You want to strike or agree?" he asked.

"Cases like this get appealed," Judge Cory said. "You'd better do it right." He looked at me. "Who do you strike, Robak?"

"Strike Judge Dermeth." He was the one I didn't know.

"Fine with me," Price said. "I'll bet I can get either of the other two here for a bond hearing within the week. Okay if I check them individually to see?"

"Fine."

He smiled triumphantly. "I'll get your subpoenas."

I waited. When he came back with them I folded them casually and put them in my inside pocket.

"I may not have to use any of these if you get all the state witnesses there," I said.

"You can bet I'll have them there," he said smiling carefully. In his mind I was sure he felt he'd manipulated me into doing things his way.

Most times, in bond hearings, the defense calls no one. But I'd decided not to do it that way. If the town and its leaders were out to get Sam I thought they at least ought to be right there in court to see it happen and answer questions about it.

CHAPTER 8

OFF AND RUNNING

I went to the track with Jeb on a bus. It departed from in front of the Grand Hotel at shortly after eleven in the morning. It wasn't packed, but it was very close to full. The bus was driven by a driver dressed in the livery of the Grand Hotel. A white-shirted waiter took orders for drinks attentively.

"You want a drink?" Jeb asked carelessly, perhaps regretting he'd asked me along. He watched me from out of the slightly crazed eyes I remembered from boyhood. He'd been the kind of basketball player who'd always outdone opponents because he did everything flat out, as hard as he could force his then thin body to go. Now he was fatter and older, but his eyes were still the same. He seemed full of confidence.

"Too early for me," I lied. I'd had earlier days. "Maybe later."

"I think I'll have one," he said to the waiter. "Heineken's please, Warren." He soon received his beer in a frosty plastic glass and sipped it contentedly.

"I go lots during the racing season," Jeb said to me, smiling at me and the beer. "It's relaxing. Going on the bus I can have a drink or three and not have to worry about driving back or about people talking."

I smiled back. "You'll probably hear it soon. I filed for a change of judge earlier today. Your prosecutor thinks we might be able to get a bond hearing scheduled as soon as next week."

"I already know about it," he said. "I heard about it within five minutes of the time you left the courthouse." He shrugged. "This is my town, remember. But all you do makes no difference to me, no difference at all."

"Maybe," I said. "But you offered help of sorts and I wanted you to know what was going on."

We smiled some more at each other. We'd not liked each other as boys and things hadn't changed, at least for me.

"Can we talk some more about Sam and your sister?" I asked.

He shook his head, still smiling. "Later. On the way back maybe. Right now I need to go over my racing form." He bent to it, flipping the pages, making pencil marks here and there.

I wasn't a complete stranger to a racing form and so I opened my own, separated the pages at the top, and looked things over. Like almost every other dullard on his way to the track I was already plotting on betting my age in the daily double. I checked. If the form sheet was right, and it usually was, it appeared my age could be two long shots. Both the first and second races were maiden races. My father had told me never to bet maidens or jumpers. I sighed and tried again to reason with myself about betting favorites without notable success. Days in the past when I'd stuck in there with favorites had always seemed to be the days when the favorites ran out of the money.

There was a special area where the buses parked. It was near the main entrance of the track. The crowd was an autumn crowd made up of diehards and aging horse players, and it was sparse. I followed Jeb down the brick walkways and we walked up a stilled escalator, he grunting with every step. We took seats at a reserved table in a half-empty dining room. Large remote television sets, strategically placed, showed the horses on the track.

"This table's our meeting place," Jeb explained, smiling again. "If I miss you or you miss me here I'll see you at the bus after the last race. Order up what you want. It's all on me." He nodded and winked. "All on me, of course," he repeated.

I had a program I'd bought on the way in. I looked it over.

"Try the five horse," Jeb said persuasively. "I had a tip on it."

After a while, after looking over the form some more, he got up and walked away.

Instead of the five horse I walked to a double window and bet my age, four and two. I then turned it around and bet two and four. Always the scientist.

I went back to the dining room. Outside the weather had suddenly worsened as some kind of front had come through. Rain fell lightly and the temperature had dropped at least ten degrees.

The television camera picked out each individual horse on its way to the starting gate. Four and two both seemed apathetic about the whole business, perhaps not liking the rain.

A waiter came past and asked what I wanted. I forsook Early Times and went to Makers Mark to impress him.

When the horses were off from the post Jeb had still not returned. Perhaps he was watching outside. I wondered why he'd invited me as I watched the nearest screen. The five horse took the lead and widened it. In the backstretch the race came up to him. As the horses dashed past the finish line I saw an unexpected sight. The number two horse had won. I waited for an inquiry sign to flash, but nothing happened. In a while the race became official and the board showed the two horse paying $39.80 to win. I vaguely wished I'd backed my choice by buying a win ticket on it and then laughed at myself for the wish.

Jeb returned to the table. He reached in his coat pocket and extracted a thick wad of ten-dollar tickets. He tossed them on the table. He smiled without humor.

"That five horse turned into a pumpkin. I've got a better lead on the four horse for the second race. The odds should be good. You might try it, Robak." He smiled at me and slapped me on the shoulder, very much the *bon vivant* instructing the country bumpkin.

I nodded. He went back to his form and I sipped my drink. Payoff possibilities flashed up for the various daily double combinations. Two coupled with four would pay $322.60.

"You going to put anything down this race?" Jeb asked, getting up.

"I've got a double going," I said.

"Which one?"

"Two and four."

He shook his massive head and laughed, calculating. "You turned your age around." He stalked off to get his bets down.

I waited at the table using my time to look over the program and the racing form. He came back just before the race and sat down, ignoring me.

The four horse led all the way and won by four lengths.

"Jesus my all," Jeb said, awed a bit. "Did you have a deuce or a ten on the double?"

"Only two dollars," I said. The loudspeaker blared instructions to double winners about locations to cash tickets, but I missed it.

"Where do I have to go to cash?" I asked Jeb.

"Fifty-dollar window. There are a couple down the stairs." He reached in his shirt pocket. His face was sweaty even though the room wasn't very warm. He sorted through a group of tickets and pulled out two ten-dollar win tickets on the number four horse. "Cash these in for me while I study the form sheet and try to figure something for the next race."

I took them from him. "Glad to oblige."

He looked down and away from me, as if he didn't want to look in my eyes.

I went on out of the dining room. I watched and listened carefully. Traffic was sparse and the wind, where there were openings out to the grandstand, was very cold. The escalator was still off, but you could walk down the metal steps and they were narrow, seemingly safer than the occasional rickety wooden steps down.

I heard the running footsteps coming behind me when I stepped onto the first step of the escalator. Whoever it was had been waiting for me to be someplace where I was alone. He came very quickly.

I took two steps down and instinctively crouched so I couldn't easily be knocked over the rail and fall the considerable distance to the hard bricks below. I turned at the same time. He tried to correct for my maneuver and I ducked further. He was muscular and quick and he used one hand to try to catch hold of me and brake his body against mine. I gave him an upward push as he went up and over me.

He was young and large. His face was vaguely familiar. I'd seen it once in a cart on the hotel golf course and again, later, in the hotel. He went desperately tumbling down the steps, out of control, legs and arms flailing. I went after him. He recovered instantly at the bottom of the escalator steps and dashed away, holding his right arm in pain. He had a hat pulled over his forehead. He was quick and agile, a very fast runner. I thought I might have endurance on him, but I was forty-two years old. I lost him around a turn. When I got up to it there were three ways he could have gone. I thought I heard a sound down one and tried it and was wrong. I came back to the point where I'd lost him and tried the others, but didn't catch a glimpse of him again. He'd vanished.

After a while I gave it up and cashed the tickets. Jeb's paid $20.80 and so came to $208 total. I shoved his money in a pocket and put my own, except for change, into my billfold.

I supposed the attacker, even if he did work for the hotel, could have seen the tickets and been after them, could have been a loser who watched for exultant, careless winners. It could have been that way, but I doubted it.

The wind was cold and I was cold. My instincts told me that going back to the dining room was not in my best interests.

I walked back to the waiting bus. My assailant hadn't ridden it or I'd have seen him. I felt nervous and light-headed, almost sick. The driver let me on with a grin. Perhaps he'd seen early losers before. I got the waiter to make me a double by buying him one also. I sat with the drink, and, later, another, and whiled away the long, cold afternoon.

I watched for Jeb. I wanted to see his reaction when he found me on the bus.

He got back on with the rest of the racing crowd. If he was surprised to see me I saw no real indication. Perhaps his eyebrows went up a tiny bit—I wasn't sure. I remembered when we'd been boys and he'd played basketball for Avalon High

School. He'd been able to do a fair job of playacting fouls. Perhaps a part of the gift had remained with him.

I handed him his money without comment and he smiled at it.

"I thought maybe you'd run into a friend from Bington or something," he said.

"I did run into someone," I said. I was all right now. The time of fear was done.

"I had a cinch in the sixth," he said. "Shame you weren't there. You could maybe have run your three up to a thousand."

"Too bad I didn't get back then," I said. "I never cashed another ticket."

He watched me carefully. I could read almost nothing in his eyes. If the attack had been a planned one, then someone would have had to tell my assailant I'd be at the races.

Another thought came: It could have been a personal thing. I probably wouldn't be much loved around the hotel now. He worked there. It could be that way, but once again I found it hard to believe.

But why attack me at all? A warning? A show of force?

"Thanks for the trip, Jeb," I said. "I'm curiouser and curiouser about why you asked me. We've never been overly close."

He smiled genially. "A number of reasons. I wanted you to go with me so that you could see how we do things in Avalon, how we live, what we do for fun. Maybe it'll help you quit thinking of us as bogeymen."

"I deal with lots of bogeymen," I said. "I've survived."

"I know that. We checked on you. They say you go right after things and that you don't give up." He shook his head. "I didn't remember you that way."

"We knew each other long ago," I said.

"Sure," he said. "There's something far more important. I talked with Senator Bratewell about you last night. He thinks you might be of use to him. I'm not that certain, but he is. I asked you to go along so we could discuss Sam and my little sister, but Bratewell asked me to do more than that. He wanted me to offer you a job in his campaign."

"What job would that be?"

"He thought if you'd agree to sign on you'd be a good man to send into the various states as an advance man as the campaign gets hotter. You could call on lawyers for him, set up meetings, drum us up some support. Bratewell's already well financed. His committee would pay your expenses and a thousand a week over that. Something else could very well rub off on you if things go well. Whether Bratewell makes it or not you could wind up with a very good federal appointment." He smiled encouragingly. "Get away from Bington, get to the big city on the Potomac where there's something happening. Maybe counsel for one of his senate committees. Something." He nodded his head ponderously, his manner that of a potentate offering largess to a beggar. "That's what he told me."

I could see the carrot. I smiled and nodded and decided to dig further into the ground that held it.

"Could I have a day or two to think on it?"

"I don't know how long the offer will be open. The sooner the Senator knows, then the better off he is and his committee is. He needs you now, Don. He needs you if you have the desire and the will to help him."

"There's Sam's case," I said.

"Someone else would have to take over. A lawyer's a lawyer."

I nodded. "I suppose that's right. I've got some very competent partners in my office who are better at this than I. One of them, perhaps?"

That idea didn't appeal to him. He made a sour face. "It might cause problems to have your partners in the case what with you working for Senator Bratewell and, of course, me. Why not just leave Sam to Ellsworthy, who's already representing him?" He held out a placating hand. "I'd promise to help hold things down. She was my sister, Don, but I'm a realist. I don't want Sam's blood, no matter what he thinks. I want it over. There's a reason that I want it over quickly."

"Could that be a possibility of the state legislature getting the Grand Hotel a local option casino law?" I asked.

He gave me a quick look. Once again I could read very little.

"Where'd you hear about that?"

"I heard about it several places," I lied. "How much blood do you want from Sam?"

"Well, it could have been an accident while they were fighting," he said softly. "Let's say I'll give Sam the benefit of the doubt and agree that it was."

"Are you talking plea bargain?"

He shook his head. "I'm not the prosecutor, the police, or the judge. I can't make you any binding offers. However, the way I'm told about the law is that such offers must be agreed to by the survivors of the victim. I'm telling you my attitude on it." He seemed almost humble.

"Thank you for that," I said. "What you're in essence saying is that for me to work for Senator Bratewell I'd have to get all the way out of Sam's case?"

"I'd prefer it that way. The Senator has a high regard for you from your time in the legislature. He thinks it would be a real coup to get you under any circumstances, but I'd rather get you squeaky clean." He smiled again at me. "It could be a real re-start for you, Robak."

I smiled back. I knew I wasn't hearing it all. Something I'd done or said had caused him/them alarm. I was an unexpected irritant. If I couldn't be cut away then maybe I could be smoothed away. Perhaps the surgical chance had happened on the escalator and now we were into plan two.

"Think on it," he ordered. "A day or two at most."

"Then see you or the Senator and let you know?" I asked, remembering my subpoenas and how difficult it might be to get at Senator Bratewell.

He nodded.

CHAPTER 9

OLD FRIENDS AND NEW

When I got off the hotel bus I went to the jail and talked with Sam again. He was eating a dinner of steaming hot dogs, baked beans, and bread off a plastic plate.

"I filed a motion for a change of judge," I said. "We probably will have a hearing of a petition to let to bail next week. Your prosecutor seems most anxious to be on with it." I nodded in the half-light of the jail. "He may not like it so well later, but he does right now."

"I've heard you were around raising hell," Sam said.

"You heard that in here?" I asked, looking around. The jail was empty except for us and one snoring drunk in a far-off cell.

"People stop past to talk—the sheriff, his deputies. People go in and out of this jail all day long." He looked around vaguely. "Lawyers, too." He shook his head and seemed to draw in upon himself, as if to be smaller. He was a man who normally, at this time of year, would have been behind bird dogs, hunting in the woods.

"I made up my mind first time we talked to do like you said, Don. Except it's got to be tried here. You make them do it here. Lots of them, including some of the local police, can't look me in the eye. They know a sloppy job was done. Some of them have kind of offhanded apologized."

"It'll get tried here, but before a special judge—one of two." I named him the two I'd left on the list, but neither meant anything to him. He put his plate down and sniffed at the jail smells. I could smell them also, sweat and urine, old, musty blankets, too many occupants on the weekends, too few the rest of the time, plus the food from a month, a week, and a meal ago. He smiled at me.

"I'll bet you got them thinking hard out there?"

I shook my head. "I don't know what they're doing. Someone tried to start a fire in your basement last night, but it was an amateur job. Someone tried to do me some damage today at the race track where I went with your old friend, Jeb Wyman. Helping you isn't conducive to sound health."

"A fire at the house?"

"Someone shoved a lighted wad of papers through the old coal chute. They burned without doing any damage. Then someone tried to push me down some steps at the track. He seemed in earnest."

"You're not afraid," he said confidently.

"Of course I'm afraid. I'm a practicing coward."

He smiled at me. He was silent for a long moment.

"The fire?" he asked. "Why would someone do that?"

"I don't know."

"Did whoever tried to push you at the track look familiar?"

I'd already made up my mind, at least for now, not to tell him any more about that. He was paranoid enough about the hotel.

"No one I knew," I said stoutly.

He nodded. "They've still got me in a tight box?"

"I suppose. Jeb Wyman said today he'd go along with a deal where his sister was killed accidentally in a fight."

"It wasn't that way."

I shrugged. "It could get things down to a year or two. Are you interested?"

He shook his head, but I wasn't sure.

"Think about it," I said.

He smiled out at me, pleased with what I'd done. "I remember when you came to Avalon with your mother. You weren't much more than a pint in size, but you had a full quart of heart when I got you away from all those books. I pushed at you and was mean to you and I'll admit it now. I kept you busy. I don't know now whether I did it because I was going through a mean spell or because we knew your mom was going to die. You needed to grow up quick, so maybe it was some of each. Me and Kate talked about it and she used to get mad at me because of how I did." He inspected me gravely. "You worked out okay."

"Thanks," I said, flattered a little despite myself.

"Go on out after them again," he said, a bit embarrassed for both of us. "And you be careful."

I went.

Outside, in the clear sunset, a light rain had begun to fall. I stood under the eave of the jail building, thinking on what to do next, thinking about Sam. When the cold rain let up a bit I walked through suddenly sodden leaves and to my LTD. My watcher was present again, parked four or five cars behind me. I walked up the street and wrote down his license number while he sat in his front seat and ignored me. License number in hand I returned to the sheriff's office.

Sheriff Bentz sat behind his desk, booted feet raised, resting them on a pullout. He eyed me inquiringly.

"Something else?" he asked.

"I've got someone following me. Here's the license number."

He took my note and examined it. He did a kind of comic double take.

"Hell, Robak," he said, "that's Lieutenant Will Hamilton from the city police. He uses his own car now and then for surveillance and stakeouts. Is he outside now?"

"He was there a minute ago when I came in here."

"Come on. You need to meet him." He smiled. "He was the investigating officer."

We walked outside. The car was still there. The man in it sat slouched behind his steering wheel. The sheriff tapped on the car window.

"Open up, Will," he said. "I'd like to introduce you two formal." He tried the knob and opened the door himself. "This here's Don Robak, Sam's attorney. And this here is Will Hamilton."

"How come you're following me, Lieutenant Hamilton?" I asked the man. He was small and nondescript with muddy, brown eyes. His coat hung open and I could see a gun inside a shoulder holster.

"I got told to follow you," he said stiffly.

"It's going to get interesting to find out, up the line, who gave you those orders," I said angrily. "The main thing, for right now, is that I don't want you following me from this time on. Continue it and I'll have you in federal court along with your Chief, whoever passed him his orders, and as far back as I can trace it. What I'm saying is that I'll sue you and your town." I nodded at him, still angry. "You ought to know what you can do and what you can't do, Mr. Hamilton. Following me, while I'm trying to do my job for Sam Hunter, isn't one of the things the law allows you to do."

He nodded. "I followed you pretty close, up where it was hard to miss me."

I realized what he meant. He'd wanted me to see him.

"Will's okay," the sheriff mumbled anxiously. He looked around, perhaps trying to see if anyone was observing him/us. "I got to go back in now."

"All right, he's okay," I said to the sheriff's swiftly disappearing back. I said it loudly and Bentz flinched and moved on more quickly.

"He's got to run next time," Hamilton explained.

I reached out a hand and, after a moment, the small man took it and shook it. He grinned out at me.

"If I'd wanted it that way you'd never have seen me," he said. "Ask the sheriff."

"I'll take your word for it. How come you wanted me to see you?"

"I had my reasons. The first is that Sam and I are, or were, friends. I still am his friend."

"What happens now?"

"I'll go back and tell them you caught me following you, tell them you said you'd see us all soon in federal court," he said, still smiling.

"Who'll you report to?"

"I file written reports. I don't know where they ultimately go. The Chief first, for sure, but I don't know much from there." He gave me an upward look. "Don't think I didn't see you go out the south door of the courthouse this morning. I saw you all right. It just suited my purpose to stay where I was." He thought for a moment. "Where'd you go?"

"Here and there," I said. "You don't really want to know, do you?"

He shook his head. "I'm afflicted with the disease of curiosity."

"So am I. Tell me what you know about Sam I don't know." I raised a hand. "I've got a copy of your original police report. Ellsworthy let me copy it."

He shook his head again. "I haven't got much else. It all stopped there, which you apparently know. I didn't like leaving it exactly where it was, but that's what I got told to do. Sam told me early he didn't do it. Sam never lied to me that I can remember. Maybe he would on a murder, but I'd like to think not. I think if he'd killed her he'd just have said so, told us why, and let it go at that. It's the way he is."

I nodded and remembered something. "Someone told me your father's on the hotel board of directors. Is he?"

"Yes. He's been on it for maybe ten years, but he don't tell me what to do or what to believe. I've done some work for the hotel, but I've also done some work with Sam."

"If Sam says he didn't do it and you believe him, then someone else did it. You have any suspects?"

He shook his head and looked away, then finally back. "That little girl liked big men. She liked to play games. Maybe she needed to feel she was being forced to do sex things. In high school I've heard she fooled with half the football team. Right before she was killed she was messing with that guy who sometimes guards Senator Bratewell, sometimes is muscle for the hotel, and sometimes follows Jeb Wyman around. I've seen some of his work. A muscle boy, a mangler. He was, I'd suppose, brutal enough for her. Abner something-or-other."

"Abner Foltz," I said. "Did you hear anything about her running with Roger Cowles, the manager at the hotel?"

"If so she was one of many. He seems harmless enough."

"What was Abner doing the night Sheila Wyman died?"

He shrugged. "I wish I knew. I did what I was told once it happened. I took my pictures and they're very good pictures which should shake up any jury. Beauty lying beaten and dead. I bagged my evidence, Sam's coat, glass fragments from her little bitty watch, and the rest. I arrested Sam." He smiled up at me. The rain had stopped. "Better ask your own questions. If you decide to question Abner then let me suggest a safe time and place. He's sometimes very unfriendly."

"Was all the glass from her watch on the floor? I mean was any of it gone?"

"I don't know. Some of it was crushed fine, like someone had stepped in it. Maybe whoever hit the girl got some of it embedded in his shoes or in the weapon. I don't know."

"Did any of it show up in Sam's shoes or clothes?"

"No. I did check that. Strangely enough I didn't expect it to show up."

"Why?"

"Because Sam said he didn't kill her."

"Anything else?" I asked. "Anything at all?"

He nodded. "It ain't all in that one report. The night Sheila Wyman was murdered a girl named Wanda Shefel came past to visit her. She wanted to borrow some money."

"That's in the report," I said.

"Keep listening, mister. Wanda said, and this is also in the report, that there'd been a fight before she got to the room, that things were still in disorder, that Sam had been mad. But she also told me she saw a scarecrow or someone who looked like a big scarecrow in the dark near the path when she left. It scared her bad and she ran. Whoever it was or whatever it was, if it wasn't anything more than Wanda's postmurder imagination, it didn't chase her or try to harm her. That ain't in the report. I got told to leave junk like that out of it."

"Who told you to leave it out?"

He shrugged, not willing to say.

"And now this girl is in Chicago?"

He nodded. "Yep. She's some leaves short of being a full tree." He made an explanatory circular motion near his head. "I think she's been on pot or booze or acid plus her back too long."

"She's professional?"

"A talented amateur, enthusiastic and greedy about her work."

"What did she do that convinced you she was crazy?"

He shook his head, unable to find correct, applicable words.

"Is it that she just doesn't, or didn't, make sense?"

"Maybe that's it," he said. "I asked around a little about this scarecrow thing even though I got told to go no further. No one else saw a thing that night."

"That night?"

"There are stories I've heard about the hotel, ghost stories. But that night no one else saw a thing. There weren't any other occupied rooms in the old wing. So I put it down to maybe drug- or booze-induced stuff. Take it and run with it for what it's worth."

"What are the other stories?"

He smiled. "I don't know them all. It's an old hotel. A lot of people have died there. So hearing it from that girl made me unsure. It wasn't anything and yet it was. Why would Sam kill the golden goose? His money was pretty much gone.

She paid for the room that night, she probably bought whatever they ate or drank. He could have her whenever he wanted her. The way I heard it she was the one mad because Sam hadn't filed for a divorce. Get it? Sam wasn't mad, she was. So what I'm doing is telling you about it. Tell anyone you got it from me and I'll wind up in trouble. I've got four years to go to retirement. Keep it away from my door. That doesn't mean you can't worm it out of me at a court hearing. It only means you can't use me and what I've said to pick at the wrong people up front of a court hearing and expect me to back you up."

I considered that and him. He'd existed a long time doing his job in the town. He knew Avalon like I never would. He'd done something for me. Before, I'd felt like Sam was being pushed hard along an inevitable corridor that led to prison. Now I felt he might not have killed Sheila Wyman, over and above the fact that the case hadn't been investigated further once they had him.

"Will you listen around for me?"

He shook his head. "No, sir. I like Sam okay and I'd help him if I could do it without problems for me. Right now I'm doing it just that way. But when I walk back into the police station and report you saw me following you, then I'll be their man again, and not yours. They don't own me, but they've got a long-term lease. If I found out something that made me dead certain it wasn't Sam then I'd say it on the witness stand, but that ain't likely to happen with the investigation completed and Sam wrapped up all pretty for Christmas. So don't expect me to be your inside man." He looked away and out his windshield, peering through the drying rain spots. "It's a tricky town, Mr. Robak, but it's my town and I've got to live here after this is done with, after you've gone. I'll do what I can for Sam within the limitations I set. One of those limitations was letting you know you were being followed and watched."

"I thank you for that."

He waited when I didn't move away from his car window.

"One more thing," I said. "I've heard that they might make some dirty movies at the Grand, snuff-type movies. Do they do anything like that there?"

He shook his head. "I think I'd know if they did. I've never heard anything about it. Some fly-by-nighter could come in and rent and use a room, I suppose. But I'd bet it ain't hotel-run or organized."

"Someone told me they got invited to a showing," I said.

"At the hotel?"

"Yes. Some remarks were made to my informant about the movie being made at the Grand."

"I suppose I could be wrong, but I doubt it. I'll still say no." He smiled up at me. "What it is is that the hotel's a place of legend, Mr. Robak. Everything important has happened there. If you don't believe that then listen to the locals. Al Capone came there, ex-Presidents used its rooms to dally with secret mistresses and play in the hot baths, millions, maybe billions, have been lost in poker games and crap games. There are ghosts and goblins and now, a scarecrow. The most of it is only legend, tall tales. Maybe it helps business. I'll ask around. If I find out I'm wrong I'll contact you again, but don't look for it."

"Thank you."

"I'll get on now." He gave me a paternal look. By warning me he'd become, at least partially, on my side. "Watch yourself. Someone else may be following you. I'll try to keep an eye on Till and Maude and on Sam's house when I can."

He seemed a good one to tell. "Someone tried to set fire to Sam's house the other night by shoving a burning bunch of papers into the coal chute."

"Kids. Or maybe not. You came into town and you began to paddle the dead horse. If anything bad happened to you, I doubt it would upset anyone around here much."

"That's comforting."

"Watch yourself," he said again.

It didn't seem too late to drive out and try to see Major Potts.

Potts was one of the good parts of my youthful remembrances of Avalon. He'd been a middle-aged man then. He'd lived two houses south of the Hunter house. He'd been semi-retired, a porch rocker, a man who'd raged at the world around him, who hated well and loudly. I'd cut his grass and raked up the clippings and listened to his complaints without really understanding them. We'd become friends in the way that fifteen and fifty plus sometimes can. He'd meticulously helped me build the model airplanes I'd constructed in stolen hours away from Mom and Sam. He'd slipped me extra spending money that winter when I'd fired his furnace by filling the coal holder in his Iron Fireman and hauling out the hot clinkers. He'd been someone to talk with, a person of use, perhaps a father figure. Judge Hunter had been cold and austere with little time for Sam and almost none for me. It was enough that he was feeding me, providing sleeping quarters, and schooling. Potts was more. He could use a few sentences and pick out the wrongs he saw in the world, make you feel them also. He had no remedies for those shortcomings, but remedies aren't always available.

He was old army, retired, then called back for World War

II, retired again soon after it. He had a string of medals and now and then he made speeches at meetings of the American Legion or the Avalon post of the V.F.W.

He'd grown up in Avalon. When I'd met him as a boy, he'd been knowledgeable about the town. His family had appeared on the Avalon scene a hundred plus years back, but after us Hunters, according to Aunt Till. She despised him because he chewed tobacco and drank liquor.

I found his nursing home after driving ten miles through the growing dark. I parked my car in the visitors' lot. A pretty, white-capped nurse inquired about my business and wanted to know what my relationship was to Potts.

"I knew him years ago so I drove over here from Bington to see him," I answered stolidly.

The lie about driving from Bington impressed her. She went away. She whispered to another, older white-cap, then vanished for a few moments. I sat in a sturdy chair and glanced out a window. The corner street light outside showed me the wet and the leaves. The rain had stopped, but it was growing colder and I thought it might soon snow. I needed my left-behind coat.

The pretty white-cap came back and beckoned to me. She murmured things about it being late, about not staying long, and about Pott's delicate condition. I followed close behind her, nodding politely at her instructions. She smelled of alcohol and perfume.

Potts lay in a roll-up bed in a small room. There was one other male patient occupant. The other man was watching the door expectantly. When I appeared he turned despondently away. Potts smiled a pink-gummed smile at me.

"Come in, Donald," he said, recognizing me instantly although it had been years since I'd seen him. "The nurse had

your name wrong, but I thought it might be you." He patted
his bed. "Sit on the end if you like, or draw up a chair."

I drew up a chair. I inspected him. One leg was gone. At
least there was nothing showing but flatness under the covers
on his right, lower side. He was extremely thin and completely hairless except for white eyebrows. His face was an
old map, with wrinkles for roads. One thing seemed the same.
His eyes were still the bright, angry blue I remembered from
my boyhood.

The room had the subtle smell of decay within it, a smell
of old, dead flowers, spilled medicine, dried urine, and
chronic sickness.

"They took the damned leg off last winter," he said conver-
sationally. "I had the high sugar and the leg split open and
there was gangrene. I could smell it. I've smelled stuff like it
before in the trenches. You never forget that smell." He
shrugged. "They sold my house and my furniture and ap-
pointed the bastard bank to pay my bills." He smiled a little.
"I don't much care. I'm just in a hurry to get through this
part of it, on to something else."

"What part is it you want to get through?"

"This last little part of living," he said, mildly irritated with
me for not knowing. "Most days now I feel like I was on an
island infested with Democrat and Republican cannibals." He
touched his bald head and then patted his mouth so that I'd
understand. "Scalped, all my teeth torn out, waiting to be the
evening feast. There was a time when I was young that I'd
get sick and not know it. Once, in France, I got wounded and
walked five miles to get help. The doctor said I should have
died." He shook his head at the puzzle. "He was right, but
premature."

He grinned at me.

"I'm glad you came," he continued. "I was going to write to you a year or two back when I saw your name in the news. Then I had a lawyer come here and I told him to make me a will, but he's not returned with it. Maybe he never will. I suppose there's not enough left to interest him. I was going to leave you something one way or the other." He reached for the drawer of his nightstand. "Can't leave anything out in sight here or it gets stolen." He rummaged around in the drawer and finally brought out a worn cardboard box and handed it to me. "Take these things with you. They won't mean much to anyone, but they still may mean a little to you. It's part of what I was leaving you, the only important part. Not that anything means much anymore. But you can look at them now and then and say the biggest coward in the world gave them to you." He smiled.

I opened the box. There were five medals inside, a glistening Silver Star, two Purple Hearts, and two gaudy French medals. I looked at them and then reclosed the box. Seeing them like this made my chest ache a little where the pinkish Korean puckers remained, made me remember again my own, aging war.

"I don't want them here anymore. The bank won't keep them, so I have to watch them. Some days I'm not so very good at watching." He nodded, looked away from me, and then back. "I know you came back because of Sam. I heard about Sam and thought you'd come back."

"What did you hear about Sam?"

"Just that he was in trouble because of that girl."

"The family wrote me and asked me to come."

"Till and Maude?"

I nodded.

"Sam's all right. Kind of mealymouthed mean, but good

enough for Avalon. He was an effective police officer for a while, until they got tired of him."

"Tell me about the town, Major. Who runs it? Who could or would have set Sam up?"

"He was set up?" he asked.

"I think maybe he was, but the guy who'd have been most interested in seeing it happen couldn't have been the chief conspirator when Sheila Wyman died."

He shook his head. "I'm long out of it, Donald. I don't know anything about it." He thought for a moment. "The hotel runs the town. It always has. You know that. It elects its people to office, it deals away people like Sam who stand in the road. But it can't stand bad publicity, continuing trouble. When Sheila Wyman died I thought Sam had done it or it was something accidental, and not meant to happen. The hotel people didn't do it, bank on that. If they had, they'd have carried the body a thousand miles away, not let it be found on hotel grounds. Dead bodies at the hotel cost money, cost conventions, cost honeymooners and hot pillowers."

"How about Senator Bratewell? How good a hold would the hotel have on him?"

"Maybe once it was real good. These days he'd be on top, big enough to deal with the hotel like he wants, but when he was in the legislature, even when he was governor, he'd have been tied into the Grand. He'd have had to be, or maybe not be elected. I'll bet he'd like to forget that now, those early days, and have the rest of the political world forget it too."

"Have you heard anything about a possible local option casino law coming in the next legislative session?"

"Only some vague rumors. I've been here in the nursing home for a long time. Would it be like the Atlantic City thing?"

"Maybe. It could mean a lot of money."

"Nowadays it would have to have Bratewell's approval. I keep hearing the hotel's losing money. They need something new to revive it. Jeb Wyman would be the quarterback. He names who runs for the house and senate seats from this district. When he pats you on your head and gets his election day people out for you, plus all the hotel workers he's got a finger on, you start way ahead. Some people beat him, but normally he then converts them." He nodded. "Or, if they're like Sam, he gets them fired or demoted."

I shook my head. "I just can't see Jeb into something where his own sister was going to get killed, something as cold as that."

"Don't ask me to figure that for you, because I've got no use for Jeb. Maybe, somehow, it wasn't supposed to happen the way it did. Once it happened then Jeb, being a realist, took advantage of the situation. Sam was still giving them fits even though he wasn't on the police. Even after the girl came along there were still letters in the various papers now and then from Sam."

"Does Bratewell chase women?"

"Not around Avalon," he said, quickly and positively. "Maybe he does discreetly in Washington. You can't trust anyone once they get there, but if Gene ever did any womanizing in Avalon I'd know it, nursing home, missing leg, and all. People still come by to gossip. Most of the ones these days are old soldiers, coming by to see me, legion boys, professional veterans." He smiled once more. "Taps players."

"Maybe Sam did do it," I said, not certain again. "He could have hurt her, killed her, when they argued and fought. She could have died. Even Sam isn't sure."

"Did you see the pictures?" Potts asked.

I shook my head.

"I did. A deputy sheriff who's a big wheel at the V.F.W. post had a set with him when he came past. That was right after she was killed and he couldn't wait to show them to me. She was badly beaten. Anyone who killed her would have known he was killing her. She was, before that, a strong girl. I saw her growing up wild. She tomboyed around the neighborhood until she had some late growth. After that there were a whole string of boys, coming and going, chasing after her. She liked them big and muscular. Wrestler types and football linemen. If someone killed her it didn't happen accidental and without the killer knowing it. Take comfort in that."

I nodded, but still wasn't sure.

We talked about old times until I saw he was tiring. I left, promising to return soon.

Outside I breathed better. The cold wind cleared the nursing home smells from my head and I clutched the box of medals. I put the box in my glove compartment and locked it.

CHAPTER 10

CONFRONTATION

I went back to Sam's house. I parked outside the shed. To hell with the possibilities of malicious damage.

The big key Till had furnished me also worked in Sam's rear door so I avoided the light-lit porch up front and the difficulties of facing Till and Maude just now. I wanted to think some more on what seemed an insolvable problem.

I moved to the front room. The chairs and the sofa were covered by sheets, but enough light came in from the porch next door for me to vaguely see. I sat on an old chair and contemplated Judge Hunter's shadowy picture above the fireplace. In the year I'd spent with him I doubted he'd said a hundred words to me, but he'd not been unkind, merely aloof, lost in his own adult world.

Below his portrait, in deeper shadows, was a cased sword. I'd forgotten its complete history, but it had been there when I'd been a boy in the house and I'd been forbidden then to touch it. Dimly I remembered that the story about it also had to do with the Civil War.

Someone tried the locked front door and then banged heavily on it.

I got up and went to the mantel and took the sword from the crumbling leather.

"Come out here, Robak," a voice I recognized called. It was Abner, Jeb's bodyguard. "Jeb wants to see you. He sent me to bring you. I seen your car out back. I know you're in there. Come on out now or I'll come through the door and it'll be worse for you."

I unlocked the front door with my left hand. In front of me, behind the screen, was Abner. He loomed up hugely in the darkness. I put the tip of the old sword against the screen and centered it on his shadow.

"Move off Sam's porch," I said. "If Jeb needs to see me you tell him to come here."

He looked unbelievingly at me and the sword. The porch lights from next door were enough to show its gleaming point. I saw there were rust spots on it further up and wondered how strong it was.

"You son of a bitch," he said, not loud, not soft.

I pushed a little and the point snicked through the screen and up against him. He jumped back.

"I hear you knew Sheila Wyman real well, Abner. I wonder if her brother knows how well? You took her to the Senator's rooms in the hotel. Maybe you did it for you, maybe for someone else. They say she liked musclemen, huge apes like you. Tell me where you were the night she died?"

"Stick it," he said. I could see the white in his eyes. He moved back a little more.

There was room enough now for me to push open the screen door. "That's a poor phrase for you to use just now. Maybe that's just what I'll do. You'll tell me sooner or later, here or in a courtroom. Why not now?"

He stepped back once more, shaking his head. "I'll tell you nothing. And Jeb still wants to see you."

"You tell him what I said."

"You're loco, you know that? Jeb could send a dozen men for you. And I'm going to watch for you and when I see you without that sticker I'm going to stomp your butt good."

I nodded at him. "Thanks for the warning. I'm going to make some calls now about that and about you, Abner. I'll tell the police and the sheriff what you said and tell them I'm taking you at your word. Under the circumstances of your threat, the next time I see you I'll be armed and I'll start shooting to open the conversation."

I could tell he believed me. He took another step back and swallowed. "Now wait one damned minute . . ."

"Get the hell off the porch, Abner, or I'll start carving some on the job now. Tell your boss there's a new judge coming for Sam's case and I'm going to change all the rules in your town. Tell him and your hotel elite and that golf course bandit who fell over me at the track today. Tell everyone in your little turkey town."

"You're loco," he said again. "I can prove I was miles away from Sheila that night. And all Jeb wants is for you not to go to his house and bother his mother anymore." He held up a huge placating hand. "I didn't mean that about beating you up. I was just hot. I take it back." He moved backward down the porch while I stayed where I was. The last time I'd carried a gun had been in a war, but he didn't know that and now I thought he'd never believe it.

He gave me one final, perplexed look at the steps, shook his head, and went down them quickly. I figured it had been a long time since anyone had defied him. He'd gotten by making muscles, crushing hands, lifting things, and talking mean. I'd made him lose some of his faith in himself. It was going to worry him. He might come back after me, he might not, but I doubted he'd ever come the way he had on this night.

I walked out on the porch to check, but Till and Maude weren't on their porch, even though the light was on.

I went back into the cold house and sat down and waited where I'd sat before, after I'd reholstered the sword. I waited a long time, but Jeb didn't come. Finally I went to bed. There were no phone calls.

I had orange juice and eggs at Avalon's edge in the morning, leaving Sam's house so early that I had to look for the earliest of the breakfast places. After eating I found a pay phone and used it to call the Grand Hotel. I had them ring Jo's room, but there was no answer. She was probably already up and out with her friend Ann Wittenberg, walking or golfing or playing tennis. The day was fine, much warmer than yesterday had been. There were no clouds and the sun had a whole blue sky to itself.

I drove past the hotel before I left town. I spotted Jo's car after I'd cruised the huge lot twice, but not Jo or Ann.

I drove out of town watching carefully behind me. If I was being followed now it was by a very good professional.

Bington was an hour plus away. I drove first to the office. Jake and the Judge were both out so I put all three secretaries to work making up discovery papers, plus a petition to let to bail, using my copy of the change of judge motion for the caption. From there on the secretaries could follow forms from old files. I had the third girl type in names on some of my presigned subpoenas.

With all three girls helping I was ready to go back in less than an hour. I left a note for Steinmetz and another for Jake. I said I hoped I'd soon be back, but I promised nothing.

I went past my apartment and got my overcoat. It seemed

silly on this fine day with the warm sun overhead, but I'd
lived cold through yesterday.

At the apartment I also checked for missing property. My
new blender was still there and so was my television set.
Things had been jumbled about, mostly my correspondence,
and the old file from the days when I'd been in practice with
now-deceased Senator Adams had been scattered about,
opened and looked over, but they seemed intact. I put them
back in some semblance of order and closed the door on them
again. I found nothing missing.

It was eleven o'clock when I started back.

I had a leisurely pub lunch along the way and arrived back
in Avalon in the early afternoon. From a pay phone I called
Prosecutor Huffman Price.

"Mr. Price, this is Don Robak. Did you manage to get our
bond hearing set for next week?"

"I did that, Sonny. Ten o'clock next Tuesday. I assume
that's all right. Special Judge DeWeese said he'd want you to
file the petition in the interim."

"I'll do it just as soon as I can get them made up," I said,
lying a little. "Tuesday, eh," I said doubtfully. "I hope I can
get ready by then."

"That was your agreement," he said coldly. "Tuesday for
sure."

"Thank you, sir," I said, and hung up.

I used the same pay phone to try Jo's room again at the
Grand, but once more there was no answer. That worried me.
When the operator at the hotel came on to inform me that
the room didn't answer I had her page Jo.

In a few moments she came breathlessly on. "What is it?"
she asked.

"You okay?" I asked.

"Sure," she said. "I'm all right if you figure that someone who had four double bogeys and an eight is okay. That's for nine holes."

"You played golf," I said brightly.

"All morning. It was lovely out there. The course was a little soft. Ann and I played with two building-and-loan-wife types. Our Indianapolis men got us into their tourney. Ann finished third and won a dozen golf balls." She paused. "I heard something funny. The building-and-loan people aren't coming back next year for their convention. First time in twenty years."

"Why not?"

"I don't exactly know. The two wives were closemouthed about it and not very happy. It was something about rates. The room rates the hotel proposed were apparently way above this year's rates."

I nodded to myself. Next year they planned to have their casino. They'd be hot after richer game than savings-and-loan conventions. They must be very sure of the passage of the casino law. I mused on that a little bit and saw a way I could use it.

"Anything else?" I asked.

"No. Oh, one more little thing, but it's silly. The hotel used to be haunted. Some say it's still haunted. There's supposed to be the ghost of a sad lady who died in a fire during the Civil War, there are two stockbroker ghosts who dived out high windows in nineteen twenty-nine, and there's a more recent goblin ghost."

"Tell me what you heard about the new ghost," I said.

"Not a lot. That's what these two lady golfers from Indianapolis were calling it. It used to wander the paths late at nights scaring people. Some people swear they've seen it, others claim it wasn't there at the same time the believers saw it."

"Have you had enough hotel?" I asked.

"I guess so," she answered regretfully. "Ann said on the golf course that she thought it was time to get back to Bington. There's a scale in the room and she was up two pounds, so she wants to leave."

"Get checked out then. Put it on a credit card and I'll give you the money for it. There's a very good reason I want you out of there today. I'm going to do some things which will cause local problems and someone who broke in may have picked up your name by digging through the correspondence in my apartment."

"What kind of things are you going to do?" she asked apprehensively.

"I'm not exactly sure yet. I'm going to raise hell. I'm going to try to use a bail hearing to investigate all the things the police didn't do."

"And someone broke into your apartment?" she asked, her voice a little lower.

"Yes. It was someone who was only interested in my correspondence. Nothing was taken. Someone just broke in and snooped." I laughed a little to make it seem trivial. "The only thing they might have found out about was you. You're my vice." I thought for a moment. "I'll want to follow you out the road and see you get started back all right."

"We'll meet you on the front porch of the hotel in an hour then," she said quickly.

"Unh-unh. Check out. Get a bellhop and have your stuff loaded in the car. Drive out of the hotel grounds and meet me on the north side of the courthouse in an hour." I stopped for a moment. "I still don't want them to know you were in there checking for me."

She giggled nervously. "I think they already know, Don. The tall gray-haired man who runs the place made a real point of buying us a lemonade when we came back in at noon after golf. He mentioned he knew you. Ann and I played dumb."

Someone checking in Bington could have found out about Jo or the someone who'd burgled my apartment could have found correspondence from her. That someone, checking further, could also soon have found she was now a guest at the Grand Hotel. So much for my attempt to infiltrate the hotel. I wondered how long they'd known. It worried me some that they did know.

"Do it now," I said.

"Okay," she said. "We'll check out."

I had an hour. I parked behind Sam's house, not bothering with the shed. I could hear noise on the front porch when I entered the gangway, so I walked curiously up to its exit mouth. Jeb Wyman sat ponderously on the porch. He was engaged in earnest conversation with Maude while Till rocked stolidly beside them ignoring them both. Abner wasn't in sight. Jeb's empty Cadillac was parked in front of their house.

He nodded coldly at me. "Been waiting to see you," he said. "Miss Maude was kind enough to invite me up on the porch for some talk." He nodded, very sure of himself and his power. "It's been a long time since I've set here. Maybe if I started coming then others would come also." He ignored Till. She seemed not to see me either. She sat with her shawl pulled tight around her, despite the warm day. She watched the street in front of her with half-closed eyes. I figured she'd not forgiven Jeb for Moll even if Maude had.

"What did you want to see me about?" I asked. "It must be real important for you not to send your strong-arm help."

"Same thing I wanted when I sent Abner to bring you along and you pulled a weapon on him. I don't want you bothering my mother."

"If you don't want that then you should have manipulated a different situation. Your sister got murdered. Your mother's going to be a witness."

"I'll send her away," he said darkly. "You're not to talk with her again."

"Send her where you want. Eventually I'll find her or a judge will order you to tell where she is. I'll depose her or subpoena her to testify, in state or out." I added a lie. "I don't need her for next week's bond hearing, but I will for the trial."

He shook his head. "It could harm her health. I can get doctors . . ."

I shrugged. "Get them if you want. I'll get mine to examine her also. It didn't seem very traumatic for her to talk to me. She was eager enough to talk about the men who'd come to the house to pick Sheila up and about you running her out of the house. Why? Did her selling it embarrass you?"

His face darkened.

Maude smiled ingratiatingly at both of us. "Sit down. Both of you ought to sit down. You're getting all heated up."

Jeb ignored her. So did I. Till ignored all three of us. I saw her pull her shawl tighter, eyes on the street.

"I'm ordering you to stay away from my mother for your good, too, Robak." He gave me a hard look. "The next time someone comes for you, then you'll not know it until it's too late for you."

"I thought maybe you set me up with a gentleman at the track the other day," I said. "I saw him around your hotel a time or two."

"What gentleman would that be?" he asked mockingly. "That was probably someone who was trying to get your attention, like Abner. The next one won't just scare you. And you won't know him or her."

I was getting tired of him. "I'll know *you*, Jeb."

"What's that supposed to mean."

"To me I guess it means you're a damned bully. You were as a kid and you still are now. As fat as you are, you probably get your sex kicks running your little kingdom of a town. You think inside your head you're still the all-American athlete, but you need help to do any job. So remember that if anything nasty happens to me or mine then I intend to blame you and come after you."

"Blame away. See if I give a damn. I may be a little heavy, but I'll bet I can still take you."

"Want to try it right now, fat man?" I asked, hoping he would.

He shook his head. "Not now. When it's the right time. If I lose then I'll have someone close to mop up." He was breathing hard, affected by what I'd said, the challenge I'd issued.

"You need all the edge you can get," I said.

He shook his head. "You and your damned cousin," he muttered.

"Someone, probably you Jeb, put the arm on the investigation of your sister's murder as soon as Sam became the principal suspect. No one in this town did a damned thing thereafter. No one tried to see if a reasonably good man, who'd spent a lot of his years as an honorable cop, was telling the truth. Now I'm going to do your job for you, fat man. I'm going to explore it all, dig in every crevice, call every witness that might help. I'm not his lawyer to roll over and play dead for you or for your Avalon. I'm Sam's man. Even if you people eventually get the job done and convict him, nobody here will like the way it happens." I eyed him and saw he was sweating a little. His eyes would not meet mine. "This is Maude and Till's porch, not mine, so I'll leave it. Don't follow me off it and don't you or your people bug me again."

"It was Sam and you know it, shyster," he muttered desperately.

"I think not and I am, by God, defending him. So you remember real well as it goes along that I'm not a part of your local processes or your power structure. I owe you and this town nothing. I owe Sam a lot."

"I'm still telling you to leave my mother completely out of it," he said.

I smiled a little. "Tell her to be ready to testify in the trial. Probably about next spring, maybe close to primary election day," I taunted. I turned my back and walked off the porch. Behind me I could see that Aunt Till had gotten up from her chair as I made my turn.

"Good for you," she said. Then she fell.

Aunt Maude screamed.

I turned back. We got her back into her chair, Maude and I. Jeb had quickly vanished. Maude went to Sam's house and called the doctor, Till's doctor.

The doctor came within minutes. He spoke to Till on the porch about entering the hospital, about round-the-clock nurses, about the care she needed.

Till shook her head feebly all the time he talked. After a time he turned to me, shaking his own head. He enlisted my aid and we carried her into the house.

It had been many years since I'd been inside. The rooms were out of an older, slower time. The rugs were thin, but they were genuine oriental. The curtains were heavy, musty and faded brocade. The furniture was old and massive. Till's bed had an honest-to-God canopy.

I went back out on the porch and waited while the doctor continued his lecture to Till. There was still time before I was due to meet Jo and Ann. I sat and rocked alone.

The doctor came out after a while. He was middle-aged. He had thin hair and a small, neat beard. His name, I'd learned, was Dr. Toine.

"It would help her a lot to go to the hospital," he said.

"I'll try to help," I said. "What is it?"

"She has cancer. She might last another month, she might not make it through the night. In the hospital I'd give her a little more time than here at home. She also has a problem heart and diabetes, but those are minor now." He looked around the porch. "She won't leave this house."

"She's lived here all her adult life."

"She'll die here. Quite soon, I'd think. In a hospital I might prolong things for her, but I don't think she cares." He shook his head at me, a little angry because I wasn't enthusiastically on his side. "She's got cancer all over. Half her insides don't work." He pointed a commanding finger at me. "You talk to her. Have Maude talk to her. I'm tired of trying."

CHAPTER 11

FINAL FORAYS

I picked up the girls at the square. If anyone was watching me or following behind me I didn't see them. To make certain things were all right and continued that way, I followed them out the Bington highway. Five miles out of town, positive there were no followers, I let them go and turned the LTD around.

I drove back to Avalon. Cars were parked in front of Senator Bratewell's headquarters. I checked his papers and filled in the dates, concealed the papers, and walked through the leaves to his front door.

Two of his guards watched me carefully as I entered. The one who'd once been a state trooper must have been filled in that I was under consideration for a post in the election push. He nodded at me. "How's it going, Robak?" he asked, grinning. "Catching any flies?"

I grinned back. "If Senator Gene is here I'd sure like to have a few words with him before I leave town for a short while," I said humbly.

"What would you need to talk with Senator Bratewell about?" he asked, winking.

"He'll maybe know. It's important and I promise it won't take more than a minute or two."

The former state trooper looked uncertain.

"Let's check you," the other guard said. He patted me down lightly for weapons. He then nodded at the ex-trooper.

"Ask the Senator," he said.

I waited for a time. There were a few anonymous others in the room, but I found a vacant chair and sat down and concentrated on my knuckles.

Bratewell came out into the room. All eyes watched him.

"What do you need, Robak? Are you going to go to work for me?"

I'd stuck the subpoena and its copy in my shirt pocket. I slipped them out and handed the original to him.

"I wanted to serve this on you before I had to leave town," I said. I put the copy back in my inner pocket.

He looked it over, beckoned me on, and led me into his private office.

"What's this?" he asked, low voiced, but angry. His complaint didn't seem to be so much directed to me as to his two guards. They hovered around, trying to see what I'd given Bratewell.

"It's a subpoena to appear at a bond hearing for Sam Hunter," I said agreeably. "Next week. Tuesday. The date's on it."

Bratewell stopped and thought for a moment. The ex-state trooper guard I vaguely knew eyed me harshly and whispered something, but Bratewell shook his head after considering it.

"Why are you doing this?" Bratewell asked. "I'm not Sam's enemy, Robak."

"I'm not calling you as an enemy, Senator. There are a lot of unanswered questions in the case. The police did no job at all to find the answers I need to prepare my case. I'm calling you as a witness."

He shook his head. "With no difficulty at all I'll bet I can find a dozen overriding reasons why I'll need to be in Washington that day, reasons why I can't possibly be a witness at your stupid hearing."

"Should you do that, Senator, then I'll release to the media a list of questions I planned to ask you. I'll make certain my release gets wide publicity."

"Why are you doing this?" he asked again, perplexed and angry.

"Your name kept recurring. One of your people, one of the guards who works for you or the hotel or Jeb Wyman, seems to have been close to the dead girl. Other people insinuate you were also."

"I very vaguely knew her is all. I know her brother very well. He's one of my people. You know that."

"That brother keeps threatening me. I think I'll be able to show he used his influence to stop the investigation after enough facts accrued to indict Sam Hunter."

"Maybe I could help you with him," he said. "Why not go after him instead of me?"

"There are witnesses who'll testify Sheila Wyman visited in rooms rented by you or your organization at the Grand Hotel."

"Not to see me," he protested. "You ought to know me better than that. My wife and I've been married for more than thirty years . . ."

"I hear also she isn't well."

"I don't fool around, Robak." He shook his head. "My reputation is spotless. It's always been spotless."

"About girls?"

He nodded.

"How about the upcoming push for a casino law?"

"About anything."

"How fine for you, sir," I said. "Congratulations. That statement from you should end all conjecture about you and the girl, the hotel, and a casino law. You tell that at the bond hearing. I mean here's this pretty young thing who got herself murdered somehow at the Grand Hotel, which is scheming to obtain a casino law. She was a girl who visited your suite of rooms there. Your thirty-year answer ought to straighten out such a minor problem. And you can just ignore the fact that the hotel where you have your headquarters is seeking a casino law." I smiled. "I'm certain the media will take no notice at all." I waited for a moment. "One way or another I'm going to keep pointing out to judge, jury, and anyone else who'll listen, that all stopped once my client was safely in jail. I'm going to keep trying to find out and then let it be known who put the arm on the local system, who his associates are, and the rest. Jeb's your man, Senator."

He watched me. I remembered him as not the most acute of men, but he wasn't stupid. Now I could see him trying the situation on for a fit, stretching and pulling at it, not liking anything about it.

"You bastard," he said softly. "You're misusing what you have."

I nodded. "Perhaps."

"Who knows you've served this or had it to serve?"

"A few quiet people so far," I lied. "Enough. No one of them is going to say anything until the bond hearing. What might help between now and then is for the police to get back into it, look hard at it again. If Sam's out of jail there's, of course, no need for any bond hearing."

"I see," he said. "Get away from me now." His voice sounded old and ill and tired.

I nodded agreeably and went to the door between his inner and outer offices.

The ex-state trooper followed me.

"Don't try to come back here again," he said softly. "He don't want you around and we don't want you bothering him anymore." He shook his head, studying me for apparent flaws. "He thought you were his friend."

"He thought I was for sale for a thousand a week and expenses," I said. "If you want to get mad at someone get mad at your buddy Li'l Abner. Or get mad at Jeb for stopping the investigation of his sister's death months back. Or maybe at the guy who works on the golf course Jeb probably sent after me." I shook my head. "I'm a lawyer trying to do a job of work. I'm not someone to be pushed, threatened, or purchased."

"Get on out," he said.

I went back outside and shuffled through the street to my LTD. In his way the guard was right. Once, a long time back, Bratewell had been Senator Adams' friend and perhaps, because of that, a little bit my friend. That had brought me nothing when I'd come into his town. I justified the served subpoena that way, but it didn't wash all the dirt away. Life isn't easy or simple and my rules weren't the controls for the game.

It was time to move quickly.

I drove from Bratewell's office to the hotel. A room clerk I'd not seen before (with only two years of service) found Roger

Cowles for me. He came out front, shook my hand cordially, and escorted me back to his office.

I gave him his subpoena. He smiled while accepting it.

"Why me?" he asked. All I could read in his voice was curiosity.

"Because I need answers. I need to ask about who owns the land near the hotel, whether the Grand is buying it or has an option on it. I need to know about an upcoming casino law, who the nonresident directors of the hotel are, where they live, who owns the stock, and where they live. I need to know how many local policemen were hired over, say the last year or so, and how much each was paid." I nodded. "Interesting stuff like that. Then I'll check it all out."

I thought a touch of red came into his face, but he remained smiling. "I was trying to help you. That stops as of now."

"Okay," I said, smiling back. "See you Tuesday."

He didn't see me to the door. When I closed it I stood outside for a moment listening but could hear nothing, no loud cursing, no frantic phone calls, but it was a thick door.

I dropped another subpoena, this one for Jeb's mother, at the sheriff's office. An officer there promised it would be served forthwith.

I drove to a pay phone and, reversing the charges, I called Steinmetz in the office.

"I'm deep into it," I reported. "There may be a bond hearing next Tuesday. I just served a United States senator and a hotel manager and the mother of the local political chairman with subpoenas. I'm no longer loved, if I ever was."

"You're a nasty man," he said, chuckling. "For your info I checked with two local realtors who were on the scene in the hotel the night of the murder. I also checked with the Ford dealer. They remember nothing at all that night except their meetings and later reading about a murder the same night they were there."

"Thank you," I said. Maybe someone had told the truth. "It was something that needed checking."

"What now?" he asked curiously.

"Just now I'm going to see Kate, my cousin Sam's wife. Then tomorrow, I'm going to Chicago." I thought for a moment. "I'm going to put my copy of the two subpoenas I served in the mail to you. Hide them someplace where a casual thief won't find them."

"How about in my filing case in the middle of the miscellaneous file?"

"Very devious, Mr. Poe," I said. "How's Jake bearing up in my absence?"

"All right I suppose." He didn't sound very sure.

"I'll see you both before too long."

Kate wasn't home when I knocked on her door, but Junior was.

He opened the door and smiled at me.

"I tried to call you," he said. "I found you a witness who'll say he saw Pop that night. It's this guy I know from my school. He was cutting across the golf course and it was before ten-thirty at night when he saw Pop."

"You didn't have to threaten the words into his mouth to get him to say them?" I asked carefully.

He shook his head slowly, but I wasn't sure.

"If you ask him to do it will he tell the police what he saw?"

"He'll tell whomever I order him to tell," he said confidently.

I had a queasy, guilty moment. I'd told him what I needed and he'd delivered.

"How come he didn't say anything before?"

Junior shook his head. "Scared or something. I don't know. But he'll say it now. He'll tell anyone I ask him to tell."

I thought about saving him back, but it wasn't the time for that if I knew the town at all.

"All right," I said. "Get him to the sheriff and Lieutenant Will Hamilton. Do you know them?"

"Sure. Is this going to do any good? Will anyone listen to what my friend says? I mean he was all by himself so there's only him."

"We'll hope they listen, Junior." I looked into the house from where I stood on the porch. "Where's your mother?"

"She went to see Pop." He gave me a smile. "Neither one of them would ask much about the other so I made up a little lie. I went to see Pop earlier today and told him Mom was coming to see him. I came back and told Mom he wanted to see her."

"That's cute," I said. "You think if they see each other they'll start talking?"

"They want to," he said. "They're both so proud neither one would make the first move. Maybe it'll happen today. If it doesn't I've got some other ideas."

"You probably would make a good lawyer," I said. "Your mother told me you spent a lot of time these days moping. Promise me that you'll get back to your books and the sports things you were good at?"

"Sure. That's easy to promise, Mr. Robak. I'll do it as soon as this gets over and Pop's out." He smiled at me. "I miss football."

"Me too," I lied.

I drove to the jail and parked outside. I waited for a long time. I thought I'd missed her.

I hadn't. Kate came out of the jail about dark. She got in an old Chevy and chugged away. I was close enough to see that she was smiling, that her head was high again. That made me feel good.

I drove to a restaurant-bar I'd spied earlier. I went inside and had two drinks and then the biggest, most expensive steak I could find on their menu, spending part of my hard-earned horse money. I had coffee and an after-dinner drink and tipped the fully clad waitress so liberally she eyed my money suspiciously when I paid. I smiled at her and told her to have a good night and winked. She followed me to the restaurant door and wrote down my license number.

I drove around the block where Sam's house was located twice, checking the area. Maude and Till's porch light was off, but there were lights on inside their house. I saw nothing else suspicious. There were cars parked on the street, but no sign of life in any of them. I parked inside the shed and locked it.

It was dry underfoot again on the brick path. I could feel the leaves powder and crackle as I stepped through them.

There were, suddenly, too many other sounds. I turned back. I did it quickly. I ran. I turned right at the exit so the house would protect me.

Someone let fly with what sounded like a cannon. It boomed behind me, probably a heavy-gauge shotgun. I heard its deadly messengers whisper to me as they passed by. I increased my pace. I saw other lights go on in houses as I vaulted the fence and cut down the alley. Whoever pursued me came to the edge of the gangway and let off one more wild shot. I was still moving, in first gear now. I stopped a hundred yards down and waited and listened. Nothing. I ran through that yard toward the street. As I exited into the front yard I heard a car start up on the street. The car accelerated screechingly away. I got to the street in time only to see receding red tail lights.

I breathed deeply, telling myself to be calm. There could be another someone waiting for me, in Sam's house perhaps, or outside it, but life is full of could-be's. I went back up the street and climbed the steps upward toward Sam's front porch. I thought momentarily about going after Jeb, but that had been mostly bluff. If Jeb had sent my newest assailant, let him worry about the possibilities of revenge.

"Is that you, Donald?" Maude called from a high window above.

"Yes. It's me."

"What's going on down there? Do you want me to call the police? Did something explode?"

"I'll call the police," I said. "Someone shot off some fireworks stuff out of season. How's Aunt Till?"

"She's better. She made me help her out to the porch for a while today. Now she's tired and sleeping. She wants to see you, but not now, not tonight."

"All right. You tell her I'll see her soon. Tomorrow I have to be out of town, but I'll see her soon." I waited for a moment and something came to me. "How come Sam's phone still works?"

Her voice was almost embarrassed. "Till said it was cheaper

to pay Sam's bill than put in a phone of our own after she got sick and we needed one." There was a pause. "If you call long distance you'll have to pay for it."

"Sure, Aunt Maude."

I heard her bang the window down. End of conversation. I went on into Sam's house warily, but no one waited there. I used his phone and called the sheriff's office. A recording cheerfully informed me that because of a shortage of funds no night watch was being kept although cars were on constant patrol. The recorder said my message would be taken at the sound of a beep. When the beep came I left a message.

I slept lightly, coming awake at each sound. The wind blew hard through the night and the house creaked and I sweated.

CHAPTER 12

BEGINNING OF THE END

In the morning, very early, long before Maude was up to tend Till, I unlocked the old shed, ran the LTD out and drove out a connecting state highway until I picked up an interstate. A lot of hours later I was in Chicago. I checked into a huge old hotel near Lake Michigan. The room I was provided was small and airless with windows which hadn't been opened since the Chicago fire. It was, however, convenient to the ice machine. I got a bucketful.

In the room closet I found half a dozen phone books. Two were yellow-paged so I set them aside. Three were for the suburban areas and the thickest one was for Chicago proper. I tried that last book first. There weren't that many Shefels and I soon found one with the same address the prosecutor had listed on his indictment witness list. Vladimir X. Shefel. I followed the pull-out directions on the room phone and dialed the number. I let the phone ring for a long time, but there was no answer.

I had a single drink in the room from my emergency Early Times bottle and then elevatored downstairs. I'd skipped lunch. I opted for an early supper and ordered a big salad and a ham, cheese, and tomato sandwich, very gourmet. After I was finished I walked outside, on across a railroad bridge, eventually coming to Lake Michigan. On my walk I was approached by one slim, lonely young lady who wanted to sell me something I didn't need. I outwalked her impolitely.

The lake was white-capped and the breeze was stiff. I saw a far-off ship. I walked along a ways, watching and thinking. Someplace in Avalon things might be going on today, soul-searching, arguments and accusations, recriminations. It was a good day for me to be gone. I wondered who'd sent the leaf-crackling shotgun man to wait for me in the gangway and whether his shots had been more warning. They'd seemed in earnest. It wasn't too early for it to have been a Bratewell supporter, but I thought him smarter than that. Getting rid of me wouldn't end his problems. Someone from Jeb? Someone else? The stiff breeze from the lake made my head hurt a little so I retreated back to my airless room.

I tried the number again. This time a man answered.

"Is Wanda there?" I asked.

"Who's this?" he asked truculently.

"My name's Robak. I'm a lawyer from south of here. I'm calling about that friend of Wanda's who was killed at the Grand Hotel in Avalon during the summer. Maybe she told you about it? I need to talk with her about it."

"She ain't here now."

"Where could I reach her?"

He laughed a little. "Don't ask me. I've been trying to reach her all her life."

"Could you have her call me when she comes in? The hour doesn't make any difference to me. Any time."

"I work, mister. I ain't usually awake in the wee hours of the morning." He liked that phrase. "Wee hours is right with Wanda."

"Then could you leave her a note?"

"I guess maybe you are a lawyer," he admitted. "You're awful damned persistent." He was silent for a long moment. "I'll leave her a note, but I'll bet you ten bucks she won't call you."

"Why not?"

He laughed some more. "It just ain't in her to do things like returning calls."

"Would you put in the note that if she doesn't call I'll come past tomorrow to see her?"

"Okay, okay," he said. "You come then. Just leave my ten in the mailbox if she don't call. She don't ever check the mail. She says it's all bad news."

"Are you her father?"

"That's right."

"Did she say anything to you about what happened in Avalon at the Grand Hotel there?"

"She says very little to me about damn anything." He hung the phone up while I was trying to formulate more questions. I hung my own up and made a silent bet with myself that he'd get no ten dollars from me.

I went back outside and wandered around that area of the city which was near the hotel, but felt I was too old for disco joints and too full of ham and cheese to eat again. When I was tired I went back to the hotel, double-locked the door, had one more drink, and went to bed. The phone didn't ring all night.

There was a persistent dream. Moll was in it, dressed in a white dress I remembered. She and Jeb were together and I watched as she fell screaming. Then time passed and she was back at the picnic, but her white dress was now dirty and torn. She seemed all right. She kept trying to tell me what had happened, but her voice was lost in the wind and the swirling leaves. . . .

I came awake fully one time only, sweating hard. I thought maybe I'd discovered/remembered something and that it had to do with Sheila Wyman and why she'd died. I thought about it for a long time.

Maybe . . .

The morning sound of trains on the elevated railway nearby was the next thing I heard. I shaved and showered and examined the remains in the mirror. Running had kept me thinned down, but I needed to get back to it on a more regular schedule. I'd lost, perhaps because of the running, my desire for huge amounts of Early Times, although now and then I still was attacked from one of my several blind sides. I seemed healthy enough but also was wise enough to admit Jo would be getting no great bargain when/if she married me (even if I took her back to the Grand Hotel for a honeymoon).

I wrote the address for the Shefel house on a piece of scratch paper and put it in my pocket. I checked out of the hotel after getting some grudging directions from the clerk, who gleefully took my money, about where the address was located.

I drove north, staying close to the lake. After a lot of blocks I turned at the street the clerk had named and headed west. I got lost one time, but a friendly filling station attendant set me aright as he filled my gas tank and accepted his bandit's ransom.

I found the address. It was an old two-story brick on a narrow lot. It looked much like all the other houses on its block. I parked in a vacant spot on the street and walked to it. There were three steps up to a bare porch. I climbed them and knocked on a thick, weathered door. When easy knocking raised no one I banged the door firmly.

The girl who finally came to answer my banging was young. Her hair was dirty blond and sleep-tousled. She was pretty in a ferret, sharp-featured way. She was of medium height and build. She blinked her eyes painfully against the daylight and eyed me without warmth.

"Are you Wanda Shefel?"

"Sure, sure," she answered in a hoarse voice. She examined me. "I seen the note when I came in. He stuck it right on my door. Did you have to make it so stinking early?"

"I'm afraid so. I've got to get back."

"Come inside then before all the neighbors see you and think you're some guy come for something else. I guess I'll have to get this over so I can get back to where I ought to be —in bed."

"That sounds interesting," I said watching for her reaction.

She eyed me with slightly more awareness. "Some other time and place," she said softly. She smiled though and reached coquettishly for my hand. I let her take it and lead me behind her into a small living room. The shades were tightly drawn, but enough light came into the room for me to look cautiously around as she pulled me behind her. No one awaited. All seemed well.

The living room reminded me of Kate's house, dark, a place to hide from the light.

"Your father's at work?"

"Sure. Him and wife number three." She sighed. "I guess I've about worn it out around here again. I'll be moving on again soon."

"Too tough here?"

"This new one's some kind of religious freak," she said. "She takes Pop with her. Every night there's a church meeting or something. She don't even believe in Christmas. She says it's pagan. She snoops in my things, probably looking for pot or pills."

"Does she find anything?"

She smiled sourly. "No. I'm high-strung. Stuff like that makes me sick anymore. I don't mess with anything these days. Sometimes I'll take a drink or three, but that's all. Sheila and I used to drink lots with that big cop that killed her. Drinking relaxes one, don't you think?"

I nodded. She had me there.

"Did you see Sheila with the big cop the night she was killed?"

"Sure. I saw her. I stopped past her room to borrow a few dollars."

"Why would you need to borrow money?" I asked curiously.

"Not for me, sir. I borrowed it for a boyfriend. He'd lost a bunch on the horses and some nasty people were after him, threatening to smack him around. I had *some* money, even though it had been a dry time, no fun or money coming in. It wasn't enough, because I was close to powdered out. Sheila had plenty and I knew that. She was easy with it." She gave me a perplexed look. "She treated it like toilet paper."

"I see. Who was the boyfriend?"

"Bobby? A guy out of Louisville. I'd take the bus down and see him some days. He wasn't from around Avalon."

"Where'd Sheila get all her money?"

She smiled. "She always had it. When she ran shy and there wasn't some man around to snag it from, she'd go home and get it from Mother."

"Tell me what you saw when you went to Sheila's room."

She shrugged. "Not a lot. It didn't stick heavy with me." She crossed long legs in a flash of white and caught her pink tongue between her teeth, thinking.

"They'd had a fight, but that wasn't unusual. She liked to run the world around her and he'd never put up with her being bossy. The room was a mess, but it usually was. They seemed okay when I was there. Sheila laughed at my jokes and listened to my excuses and gave me a twenty. Sam hugged me and gave me a drink. They weren't angry, really angry. I'd seen them fight lots without it meaning anything. They'd get into it and over it quick. She was a feisty girl and, like I said, she'd start things if it wasn't all going her way."

"So you borrowed your twenty, had a quick drink, and moved on. Anything else?"

She shook her head.

"One of the police told me there was something about a scarecrow or goblin or something. He told me you mentioned something about seeing it on the hotel grounds?"

"I never really saw a thing," she said. "It could maybe have been someone in the bushes making love. They do that now and then. With hundred dollar rooms they get drunky and make lovey where they fall. Or maybe it was a dog and a shadow across the moon." She shrugged. "I'd had a couple of earlier drinks. I heard something and saw just a flash of something."

"Tell me what it looked like—what you saw."

"Nothing human. Three legs or more. Running in the bushes. Big and quick. I was afraid. I'd heard all the hotel ghost stories. I ran. I found a door into the hotel and went down to the downsteps bar and had a quick drink and then it was okay. I told the barman about it and he told me to change my brand and we both got a big laugh out of it." She shook her head. "Next morning Sheila was dead. And now here you are in my front room asking lots of questions." She eyed me and I thought maybe she was losing her feeling this wasn't the time or place.

"I'm real late," I said, looking at the clock on the table. "I've got to see someone else and get back." I smiled to show how regretful I was and she shrugged indolently. "How close were you to Sheila?"

"That night or all the time?"

"Both."

"We were as close as sisters. I went with her lots of times when she was sneaking on old Sam. I doubled with her." She shook her head, perhaps remembering the good times. "She could be a wild lady."

"Who else was she dating?"

"It might be easier to ask who she wasn't dating." She thought for a moment. "There were plenty of men around. She fooled with the hotel manager a little, but she claimed that was platonic. I guess it was. I went out with him once and nothing much happened. She went with that big guy Abner who was some kind of go-between between her brother and the hotel and Senator Bratewell. I guess they all used him because he's so big and mean. She went out with hotel guests, townsmen, hotel workers. But around the time she got killed it was mostly Sam. He didn't leave her a lot of time for anyone else. She was jealous of him and afraid to do much and he watched her pretty close."

"Did she do anything with Senator Bratewell?"

"She never said so and I imagine she would have bragged if anything had been happening there. She wasn't real secretive about her love stuff, at least with me, and the Senator's dreamy. Sometimes that Abner used to try to get her to slip into the Senator's suite with him when no one was around and Sam wasn't watching, but I figured that was for Abner himself."

"Did she and Sam argue the night you were there?"

"Some. She'd not been someplace where she was supposed to be when Sam came looking. He then wound up in one of the downsteps bars and she had to go looking for him. He was mad, she was mad. But I thought it was over when I left them. They were all sweetness, kissy-kissy."

I kept it up for maybe ten minutes more, but there was nothing else. At the door, when I left, she smiled at me.

"You come back, hear? You call me sometime when you have more time." She nodded at me, sure of herself. "We could have fun."

I wondered if she'd mind if I brought Jo along, but decided not to ask.

"If I wanted to do that, with you talking about moving on, how would I get in touch with you?"

"Pop'll have my address. He always has had my address. Everything I know I learned from him." She gave me a bitter smile.

I had no intention of asking her questions about that. One problem at a time.

"One more thing, Wanda. Did you ever hear of anyone making any movies at the hotel?"

"Now and then some guy would want to take pictures—some freak."

"I don't mean pictures or regular dirty movies. I mean 'snuff' movies. Do you know what they are?"

"I know." She shook her head. "Some of the girls used to do posing, but it wasn't an organized thing. Once I got asked by some cuckoo who came into the hotel in a Rolls to act in a movie. Some of the other girls were in it also—just girls and this one guy. But it wasn't any snuff stuff. I never heard of anything like that."

I got back into Avalon in the late afternoon. I parked the LTD in front of Ed Ellsworthy's law office building. I walked up his dark steps and entered. The pretty young secretary was absent from her desk so I tapped on Ellsworthy's inner door. I could hear something inside, but no one came to the door so I opened it.

He eyed me for a moment without recognition. When he knew me he smiled.

"Robak, my boy," he called. "I've been trying since this morning to trace you down."

"I drove to Chicago to talk to Wanda Shefel."

He nodded abstractedly, not caring much apparently. "I've got bigger news than you seeing a witness. It seems Sam's suddenly pretty much off the hook. The prosecutor and the city police have called here looking for you also. A new witness turned up, a kid who claims he saw Sam on the golf course moving away from the hotel prior to ten-thirty the night Sheila was killed. Everyone seems upset and earnest about it. They've reopened the whole case. Apparently, until there's definite proof over and above what they now have against him, they're going to turn Sam loose. That hasn't happened yet, but they say it'll happen soon, tonight or tomorrow. They're now looking for a man named Abner Foltz who worked around the hotel and who's disappeared."

"Does Sam know about any of this yet?"

"I've not talked to him. He's probably heard something. That jail's a sieve. I thought maybe you'd be the one to tell him what's happening." He came over and put his old dry and cold paw out and we shook hands gingerly. "How'd you do it?"

"Do what?"

"Get them to start looking again? Get them to look at anyone other than Sam?"

I shook my head in staged bewilderment. "I don't know anything about it."

I could tell he didn't entirely believe me. He let go of my hand and drew his own back.

"All right. I know a little. This new witness? He's the one found by Sam's son?" I asked.

"Yes, but there's more to it than that. After he turned up, the police started asking other questions, talking to other people, and the chief bellman at the hotel thinks now he saw Sam out there crossing the course leaving the hotel also. He got off at ten o'clock and he's told the police he was out picking up his car long before ten-thirty. He saw someone on the course and he's told them he thinks it was Sam."

"I see." I remembered hearing about the chief bellman. He was the one who'd led the secret meeting in which oaths had been sworn that Sam would be found quilty. *Easy come, easy go.*

"The prosecutor told me he wanted Sam to plead guilty to assault. He'd get a ten-buck fine and the time served to now as his sentence. That'd tidy it up for all of us." He gave me a satisfied smile.

I went to the jail. The sheriff sat at his desk doodling cars and airplanes on a yellow pad.

He smiled up at me. "I thought maybe you'd be around before the day was over. I keep hearing there ain't going to be any need for a bond hearing for Sam, that things have changed, that Sam's an innocent man. Prosecutor was in here earlier, but he was some kind of grumpy, wouldn't let on what was happening, and told me to butt out. He seemed kind of upset. The locals called us and said to pick up Abner Foltz if we saw him. I guess there's a warrant out for him, but I've not seen it."

"Can I see Sam?"

"It's after visiting hours, but I'd let you in if I could come along and listen in?"

"All right. Did you know someone tried to burn his house one night when I was staying there? It was a poor job."

He shrugged, not particularly interested. "Kids probably. The park's close-by. They've given Till and Maude some problems. We send a car past now and then."

I nodded. "And the shotgun man?"

"You tell me."

"I thought maybe someone from the hotel. I had a run-in with one of the golf course people down at the race track."

"You want to file papers against him?"

"No. It was out of state."

"All we found were some skinned places in the bricks. I'd guess he was shooting buckshot. You're lucky he missed." He thought for a moment. "You ought to be safe now. I'd imagine the hotel will be glad to have you gone from town."

I thought that was probably right.

He turned and led the way. The jail was fuller than it had been when I'd been inside it the two times before. Half a dozen prisoners called out to the sheriff. They wanted cigarettes, telephone calls, lawyers, family, and friends. Most of all, they wanted out.

Sam sat on his bunk and watched our slow procession.

When we arrived, I said, "I don't want to give you any false hopes, Sam, but there's a chance you'll be outside this place soon."

He got up and came to the cell door. He shook his head like a dazed fighter. He slid a huge arm through the bars and clamped onto my arm painfully.

"How soon?"

"I'm not certain. I've heard a day or two."

"How'd it happen?" he asked.

I shook my head. "I'm not certain about that, either. I went to Chicago to talk to Wanda Shefel, Sheila's girl friend. When I got back a while ago I found out what was happening from Mr. Ellsworthy. He said they found a couple of witnesses who saw you away from the room before the time they think Sheila was killed. One of those witnesses your son Junior turned up for you. The other's a hotel employee." I held up a hand to stop his questions. "The way Ellsworthy explained it to me they'll still want you to plead guilty to assault and that'll be a part of the deal of getting out. No more time and a ten-dollar fine."

"Sure," he said. He smiled. "Okay by me." He smiled more. I could almost see him working it over inside his head, refusing to inspect the gift horse. "I'll do whatever they say to get out. If Kate'll take me back, and she says now she will, I'm going to move on with her and the boy. That'll give the town out there time to forget us and us time to forget the town."

"The town will never forget, Sam," I said softly. "Like that Civil War soldier who came back home and burned the hotel, you'll be a permanent part of the Avalon legend."

He looked me over, unsure of my meaning, but beside me the sheriff chortled, "That's right. That's perfect right."

"Who killed her, Don?" Sam asked, like a curious child.

I shook my head. "I don't know for certain. You were my job, Sam. With you out of jail and safe, I'll go back to Bington. I'm going to get married soon. I'd hope you and Kate would come over for that. I've got a lot of work to do there, too." I turned to the sheriff. "I've got one thing I want to ask Sam about in private, Sheriff. Would that be okay? It's personal and not about his case."

"Sure," he said, inclining his head. "Sure. That's okay with me." He moved a little away.

I leaned forward and whispered, "Sam, when we were kids and I was living in Avalon in your father's house, were you and Katie lovers?"

"I've always loved Kate."

"I know that. But did you make love, physical love?"

He drew back a little. "Why do you want to know?"

"I've a reason. Humor me."

He shook his head slowly. "We never did it until we got married. I swear it. I wanted to. At times Kate wanted to. But it never worked out. So we waited."

"Thanks," I said loudly. "Come back, Sheriff. Sam owes you a lot of gratitude for being of help to him."

That occasioned more hand-shaking between Sam, the sheriff, and myself.

When I left the sheriff stayed behind at Sam's cell door. He and Sam were into hunting-fishing stories, very intent about them, arguing amiably now and then.

CHAPTER 13

THE END

The sun was almost down when I stepped onto Aunt Till's big porch. The fall wind was cold against my face and the sky above was a combination of pinks and blacks and grays.

Maude wasn't in sight, but Till sat on the porch rocking weakly. She wore an old, warm sweater, gone a bit at the elbows. She had her long shawl pulled tight around her.

"I'm glad to see you feeling better," I said. "Where's Aunt Maude?"

"She went to the store. Jeb Wyman came past and offered to take her in his fancy car. He was nice as a piece of warm lemon pie. He left a note for you. I've got it here."

She handed it to me. The envelope had been opened. The note read, "Mail your copies back to me."

"Did you read it?" I asked.

"He said I could," she answered defensively. "It didn't mean a thing to me. What does it mean?"

"Nothing much. I'll be leaving in the morning. Maybe yet tonight."

"I thought you'd be staying to help Sam," she said plaintively. "The radio said there was some kind of hearing set for next week." She moved a little to face me better and I could see the movement caused her pain.

"There isn't going to be any hearing or any trial. Sam will be getting out of jail. Tonight or in the morning. The police now think it was someone else who killed Sheila Wyman."

"There ought to be a trial," she said fretfully. "How can things be done for Sam without a trial."

"Sometimes it works out that way."

She leaned toward me from her chair and her eyes narrowed in pain.

"Are you okay?" I asked. "You ought to be inside or, better, in a hospital like your doctor said. It's cold out here."

"I'm just fine. I hurt a little from my rheumatism. That Dr. Toine's crazy. I always get to feeling bad when the leaves come down and just before the first snow. I think it's something in the air, leaf dust, dead grass, something. This year it's been worse with no one stopping past, with the town quitting on us because of Sam and what he did to that dead girl." She moved around, seeking a more comfortable place in the chair. "I'll be around for a long, long time yet."

I could see she'd visibly lost flesh even in the few days I'd been in town.

"How's your appetite?" I asked.

"It gets my appetite, too," she admitted grudgingly. She looked out at the street. "Since I stopped walking seems I just have to be out here on the porch, see my town parade by, see my friends, even if they aren't my friends anymore."

"I remember you walked," I said. "When was it you stopped?"

"Not long. Not long at all. I still like to walk a little on days when I feel good."

"Wearing your long shawl and carrying your big cane?" I asked.

She nodded.

"Did you walk the night Sheila died, Aunt Till?"

"I don't know. My memory for times is real bad. I'd guess not."

"I'll bet, if I tried, I could find someone who saw you that night. Maybe walking, maybe later hiding in bushes and trying to see bad things. Walking tall and thin, with the shawl hanging down, flying in the wind, and the cane." I reached over. The cane stood beside her chair. I picked it up. She hadn't used it a lot recently. The rubber tip at the end seemed gritty. I rubbed it and lightly scratched my finger. "They say bloodstains can show up after a long time, Till. I'll bet a test would show them."

"The wind out here's beginning to bother me some now," she said. "Could you help me inside?"

"In a little while."

"Don't ask me any more silly questions," she said. "It makes me feel weak and faint when you ask such crazy things."

"I think maybe you got Moll, too," I said. "What was it? Did you see her and Jeb making love out there at the state park? Did you follow her and use that cane to push her off the cliff? You told me that first day when I came back and sat on your porch that Moll had screamed that night and fallen from the cliff. How could you know she'd screamed unless you'd been there?"

"I don't know anything," she said logically. "If you fell off a cliff wouldn't you scream?"

"Perhaps. But I thought maybe you heard her. What was so bad about Moll?"

"Nothing was bad about Moll. She was a wild girl, but nothing was bad. And you have nothing to prove what you're saying," she said primly.

"I've a few things. Maude sent for me. You're the head of

the family. The world knows you dominate Maude. You didn't send for or want me here. You warned me not to talk to Jeb's mother, but I did, and she was all right and a help. You and Maude, in the meantime, have become outcasts on your porch, but you weren't fighting back, you weren't raising hell. You didn't want me to talk to Major Potts, you told me to move on. You wanted Sam punished."

"He should be punished," she said severely. "I can find you some passages in my Bible. He should die, too. But if they say it wasn't him then maybe it was one of those hotel people." She smiled. "Maybe the same one who shot at you. Maude and I saw the sheriff looking around. He told us what had happened."

"If it had been a hotel person my bet is that Sheila's body would never have been found, Aunt Till. If it had been the hotel or Bratewell, the body would have been in concrete at the bottom of the river."

She leaned toward me, old eyes fierce. "I snuck up the back steps one night," she whispered. "I saw those girls dancing nude. People who'd do that would do anything bad. Sam was in there watching and sitting and touching that girl."

I shook my head. She nodded hers positively. A standoff.

"The final thing that clinched it for me, although I didn't know it was you yet, was when someone tried to fire Sam's house. Right now I'm guessing you saw me take my Jo in there. It set you wild. You imagined what we were doing, that dirty stuff. We had to be punished, too. So you built a little fire out of newspapers in the gangway and pushed it down the coal chute. A pitiful little fire."

Her old lizard eyes closed. She leaned forward painfully in her chair.

"I must get in. I'm chilling."

"All right," I said. "I'll take you inside now, Aunt Till."

"Who have you told all this silliness?" she asked carefully.

"No one. Not yet. I don't know exactly what to do yet."

She nodded weakly. I handed her back the cane. I got her left arm and helped her up. I opened the door and smelled the odors of the old house. Dust and must and rust. I got her inside and closed the door behind us.

She remained stronger than I'd thought she'd be. She waited until I let go of her arm and then she stepped away a little. She swung the cane around as hard as she could. I was watching and tried to catch it, but missed. It caught me on the side of my head and I saw stars. I'd wanted her to do what she was doing, so I could be sure, because I wasn't sure, but I'd not wanted it to come out so well for her.

I staggered away. She swung again, this time futilely, missing me, losing her balance. She fell.

I got her up and to a chair. I sat her in it. She was sobbing. I could not remember ever seeing her cry before.

"Bastards, bastards," she muttered. "All the world's full of filthy bastards . . ."

"Sure, Aunt Till." I felt my head. There was a small lump, but it didn't seem that bad.

"What are you going to do?" she asked. "What are you going to say?"

I shook my head. I'd known her almost all my life without ever knowing her at all. I owed her no answer, but I gave her one.

"I'm going to take the cane. If anyone else gets picked up for Sheila's murder I'm going to tell the sheriff everything. Maybe I'll do it anyway. I'm going to think some on it."

"I'm an old woman," she wailed. She produced her Bible

from someplace and waved it at me. "I've been a good woman."

Outside, when I walked down the steps to the street, after I'd packed the few things I still had at Sam's house, I saw Jeb pull up in his big Cadillac. Aunt Maude got out. Jeb came around to assist her.

"You tell Sam I helped him," he said to me. "You tell him that. And I want your subpoena copies. I want all of them. I'll get the one from the sheriff on my mother. I want the other two bad. I need them or I'm out of a job. Maybe I'm out anyway. Gene's not happy. They don't come in the mail in a few days and all bets are off."

"Before anything goes into the mail Sam will be out and the matter of your sister resolved with prejudice to the state."

"Sure," he said.

"Then I'll mail them." I looked out at the car. "What did you do with Abner?"

"Gone. Disappeared. It's been two days now."

"You sent him after me with a shotgun, didn't you, Jeb?"

"Not me," he said.

I thought he had. My gangway assailant had fled as if he thought I was armed. Only Abner would have thought that.

I moved past him and he backed out of my way.

I said, "I wonder if they'll ever find Abner, Jeb?"

"I wouldn't know anything about that," he said.

Aunt Maude said, "You've got Till's cane."

"She gave it to me," I said. "A going-away present. Goodbye to you, Aunt Maude."

She nodded at me and her eyes were fearful. I wondered what she knew and suspected about Aunt Till.

"Good-bye," she said.

I got in the LTD. It was the first time I'd ever parked it in front of the two houses.

There were others in pursuit of Senator Bratewell. Let them settle his problems among themselves. I had no idea what he knew, what he'd done. I'd only used him as once, when I was in the legislature, he'd used me.

I drove out the road and toward Bington, my own town. As I drove a soft, first winter snow began to fall, melting on the highway, but coating the ground in pure, shimmering white.

Joe L. Hensley has written for many science fiction and mystery magazines and is the author of seven previous Crime Club novels including *Song of Corpus Juris*, *The Poison Summer*, and *A Killing in Gold*. He often draws on his extensive legal experience, which includes a term as prosecuting attorney for the Fifth Judicial Circuit of the State of Indiana. He was recently elected to a judgeship.